Saving Grace
EM Chandler

EMCHANDLERBOOKS.COM

Kissing Chaos: A Havenwood Novel

Copyright © 2025 EM Chandler Books LLC

All rights reserved. No part of this book may be reproduced or transmitted in any form or by any means, electronic or mechanical, including photocopying, recording, or by any information storage and retrieval system, without permission in writing from the author/publisher.

This book is a work of fiction. Names, characters, places, and incidents are the product of the author's imagination or are used fictitiously. Any resemblance to actual events, locations, or persons, living or dead, is coincidental.

Editing by Andrea Halland, Editing by Andrea

Cover Design: Ever After Cover Design (Acacia)

To the moms, no matter what your situation looks like. Even when it feels impossible to go on, remember this: You are brave. You are strong. You are loved.

You've got this, mama.

To my grandmother—Thank you for being one of my biggest supporters.

This is the second book in an interconnected standalone series. You do not need to read *Kissing Chaos* prior to this book. However, *Saving Grace* does contain spoilers pertaining to the first book in the series.

Content Warning

Pain pill addiction/recovery (no on page use)

Panic/Anxiety (on page)

Secret baby (on page)

Loss of parent(s) (off page)

Mild discussion of gun violence and trauma related to bullet wound in FMC (incident occurred in the past, not on page)

Mild discussion of infertility/adoption/fostering relating to secondary characters

Contents

1.	Leila	1
2.	Drew	10
3.	Leila	27
4.	Drew	34
5.	Drew	41
6.	Leila	48
7.	Drew	54
8.	Leila	63
9.	Leila	70
10.	Drew	79
11.	Leila	85
12.	Leila	95
13.	Drew	100
14.	Leila	114
15.	Drew	120

16. Leila	124
17. Drew	149
18. Leila	155
19. Drew	166
20. Leila	174
21. Leila	180
Epilogue – Drew	189
Have you read Jett and Noah's story?	195
Chapter 1	197
Acknowledgements	211
Thank you for reading!	213
Works by EM Chandler	215

Chapter 1
Leila

"Are you sure about this?" my older brother asks as he leans against my bedroom door. Gavin's six-foot frame takes up most of the opening, the worry in his eyes something I've come to know quite well over the last several years. I'm the one who usually puts it there, after all.

I offer a smile that is hopefully more convincing than it feels, especially since my insides are twisted into so many knots that I think I might actually make myself sick. "I'm going back to Havenwood, Gav," I say, breathing through the nausea. "It's the right move."

The only move, really. The last several months have been nothing short of terrifying, but by some miracle, I'm still standing. Hell, if I'm honest, the last decade has been one gigantic nightmare after another. But the little girl in me, the one who remembers the feeling of belonging, of safety, wants to find that joy in life again.

Especially now.

Gavin runs his fingers through his nearly black hair, the locks just long enough to stand on end when he does it. "You may not like what you find when we get there," he warns.

I glance around the room, making a show of its emptiness with one arm stretched wide. "You do realize this room is void of all personal items, right? We've already loaded up the moving truck with everything we own. I'll figure out our living situation once we get there. I know you'd rather not get woken up at all hours of the night."

He stands tall, stretching to his full height like it'll give him the power to sway me. "You're staying with me, Leila. There's no point in you paying rent somewhere when you don't need to." Glancing down at the bundle in my arms, he adds, "Maybe we should wait a few more weeks."

I shake my head at the big oaf. He worries too much. It's justified—I'm a walking panic attack—but he put his life on hold for me. It's been ten years since Gavin carted me away from the cause of my night terrors, leaving our hometown

"Unless you plan to convince Kaia to accept formula for the first time when she wakes, you can't take that one right now," he says while holding his hand out for the canister. I willingly place it in his open hand, and he turns his focus back to the road as the light turns green. "Everything is going to be okay. Try not to create issues that don't exist yet."

Rolling my eyes, I huff. "Just a few hours ago, you were arguing otherwise."

"Yeah, well, we're almost there now. So, buckle up, buttercup."

I take a deep breath, trying to cleanse the ensuing panic from my system. He's right, of course. My mind is conjuring all the possible ways this could end badly.

When I still don't say anything, Gavin sighs. His fingers slide up and down the steering wheel, his own anxious tell. "What's going through your head right now?"

"What if I can't do this? What if being back here triggers too many memories? What if this is all too much, for everyone?" For Drew, but I don't say that part out loud.

I know the words my brother wants to say are along the lines of *Where was this hesitation before I called Kelsey?* but he's a good sport about it. He knows it's just my anxiety talking. I haven't stepped foot in Havenwood in a little over a decade. I never came back, because the trauma inflicted by my mother and stepfather was too great. Every happy memory I'd ever had here had been wiped away by the trauma and heartache they brought to this sweet little town.

Back then, Gavin was in his twenties and lived in our dad's old house. By the time he caught wind of the situation, it was too late. I was a shell of my former self, the happy-go-lucky child that never met a stranger. The bullet wound in my arm was luckily the worst of the physical damage done to me.

I can't say the same for my egg donor and her dealer.

"You need to breathe, Leila," he says, his tone as firm as the grip on my arm. His touch serves its purpose, grounding me from the memories that are trying to burst from their cobwebbed crates.

As my eyes take in our surroundings, a sleepy whimper sounds from the backseat. Luckily—or unluckily, depending on who's asking—we've made it to the outskirts of town, where our dad's old house sits. Gavin must have pulled into the drive while I was lost in my head.

The white one-story ranch house with black shutters and a matching front door isn't much size-wise, but it's plenty big for the three of us for now. Gavin steps out of the SUV and opens the back door, unlatching the car seat from its base and bringing Kaia around to my side. Her eyes are still shut, but her little fists are bunched tight. She'll be starving when she does wake. We stopped once about ninety minutes in, but she slept the remainder of the trip.

Glancing around, I recognize one of the ranch's trucks on the street and count my breaths while looking only at the tiny human. If I don't see the Flynn brothers, then they aren't there...right? Please let it be the older brother. I'm not ready to face Drew yet. I just need a few hours to settle in, and then I'll hunt him down. Maybe.

It's been eleven months since I laid eyes on Drew, when he made it clear that we couldn't keep doing this. Whatever *this* was. We'd been on and off in secret for years, only getting together when he and his brother Declan visited Gavin on their way to pick up horses in Kentucky. He'd told me he loved me. And I had been naïve enough to believe him.

Things are different now. I'm not here for Drew. Not really. I'm here for Kaia.

And with that thought, I steel myself for the heartache that is sure to come.

Chapter 2
Drew

The neon sign flashes in the window as I hesitate outside the door of Riley's Bar and Grill. The person on the other side of that door may be my best friend, but I can already feel the ass chewing he's about to serve up.

I take a breath and hold it before exhaling and going inside. It's best to get this over with.

As soon as I enter, I spot Jace. He's built like a linebacker and impossible to miss. He always attracts the ladies, and at first, I think today is no different as a brunette drapes herself over the bar. On second look, I realize it's our friend Jett trying to reach the ketchup bottle there.

heard my scream during the start of a particularly rough nightmare-turned-panic attack.

Walking in on your brother and your best friend's sister while neither are clothed leads to questions no one wants to deal with.

My knee bounces against the glove box, and my knuckles turn white with their grip on my phone as I try to bring my focus back to the e-book I've been slowly working through. Usually, Laura Beth's medical romances are my bread and butter, but I can't slow my mind enough to focus on the snack of a doctor who falls for the nurse who works three jobs to stay afloat.

I glance in the backseat again, forcing a deep breath as I take in Kaia's sleeping form.

Turning back to the front, I set my phone in the cup holder, clenching my eyes closed as I drop my head into my hands. Blunt nails press into my scalp as I massage it roughly. I take a breath and open my eyes, shaky hands reaching for the center console as Gavin slows for a traffic light. I fumble through all the junk until I find the emergency bottle of anxiety medication.

I shake it twice, the sound of a single pill bouncing around soothing something inside of me. As I try to remove the lid, Gavin places a hand on my unsteady ones. I look up to meet his concerned hazel eyes.

***

The journey from Tennessee to Georgia is a long one of mostly mountainous roads, the Blue Ridge Mountains stretching a good portion of the trip. After nearly three hours on the highway, my anxiety reaches its max as doubts double down on the good vibes I had going.

Gosh darn it. Maybe this isn't the best idea.

When I reached out to Kelsey Riley a few months ago about finding a way to come back home, I left out the fact that we'd have a baby in tow. She knows now, of course, because Gavin can't keep anything from his ex-girlfriend, but that's a story for a different time.

And while I may have let Gavin believe otherwise, Drew hasn't answered a single text or call since the day Kaia was conceived and he shoved his big brother out of our hotel room. He closed the door between us that night, in Tennessee and in our relationship.

It's not like Drew would have told anyone about us anyway. We'd kept our relationship a secret before the pregnancy. With our brothers being best friends and work buddies, we didn't want to muddy the waters between the two. Especially since we lived in different states.

The only reason either brother found out we'd been sneaking around for the last several years is because Drew's brother

"I'll load up the last few bags. We can be there before lunch if we leave soon." He hesitates before adding, "Did you give anyone a heads up that we're coming into town?"

Nodding, I shrug. Not a confirmation exactly, but...

"I sent a text. You know how hit or miss things have been, though. I think he needs this as much as us. We need a support system. What better place to find one than in the best little town in Georgia?" At least, I hope that's what we find. This idea has more potholes than a southern backroad.

"Your heart is too big, baby sister. I hope Drew doesn't break it," Gavin says as he walks out to put the rest of our bags in the already running Explorer. The *again* that he keeps to himself rings clear.

Glancing down at the bundle in my arms and placing a kiss on my seven-week-old daughter's head, I sigh and soak up the newborn snuggles as she snoozes against my chest. "You and me, both," I whisper to Gavin's retreating form as I hold Kaia close and silently pray that I'm not making the worst decision of her tiny little life by taking her closer to family.

To her father.

To the one man who loved me through all the ups and downs before crushing my heart into a gazillion pieces.

To the cowboy who calls me "sunshine."

The one and only, Drew Flynn.

and his life behind. When the opportunity presented itself for him to move back and oversee farm operations of River Haven Ranch, he wanted to say no. With everything that happened in the last year, he wanted to stay in Tennessee. For me. For my sanity.

I understand his hesitation. I swear I do. He doesn't want to see me hurt again. *I* don't want to get hurt again. I don't have time to go through the constant tears and feelings of inadequacy again, but staying in Tennessee is only masking the problem.

I'm done hiding from my past.

Slipping the band from my hair and undoing the tangled braid, I offer my brother a gentle smile. This one at least feels sincere. "It's all good, brother. The doctor said everything looks good, just to take it easy. And I already have an appointment set up with Kristen for next week to keep my therapy sessions flowing like they suggested."

When he opens his mouth to argue, I hold a hand up. "We're going back to Havenwood, Gavin. My mind is made up. And you know damn well you won't be able to change it."

My brother sighs heavily, clearly conceding to my victory. Not that it's anything new. I'm nothing if not stubborn to the bone.

"On that note, I'm heading back to work. Kelsey needs to duck out in a bit, and there's a new frozen coffee recipe she wants me to try," Jett says, already backing her way through the tables to avoid the impending confrontation. "Tell Noah I'll see him at home when he finishes helping you." She runs into a table corner but doesn't flinch as she waves at us, her focus already on the little bookstore and café she and Jace's twin own across the street. They opened it a few months ago, and the place has taken off. Kelsey runs the café side, creating off-the-wall coffee drinks and pastries, while Jett runs the bookstore and author services side.

Once she steps through the door, Jace turns his focus back to me. "Rough day riding ponies?"

I nod. "This heat is going to be the death of me," I say before taking a sip of the cool drink in my hand.

Jace chuckles. "You've lived here your whole life and you still aren't used to August in Georgia?"

I roll my eyes, my lips quirking up on their own accord. "Being used to it doesn't mean I have to like it."

The humidity has been its own version of hell lately. Imagine taking a hot shower and then putting on long sleeves and jeans without drying off first. That's what Georgia humidity feels like.

"Well, look what the cat dragged in," says another voice from the back room. I glance up to see Noah Slater, our other best

I slip behind the bar unnoticed and grab a glass and a bottle of whiskey before pouring two fingers and taking a seat on the other side of the bar, closest to the jukebox that hasn't worked since we were kids.

Jett still hasn't noticed me, and I'd usually give her a hard time about her lack of awareness, but there's too much on my mind today.

"Hey, man." Jace's deep voice startles me as it booms across the empty bar. "I'll be there in just a second. Gotta get this shipment put away real quick."

I wave him off, but his words pull Jett from her current fixation.

"Hey, Drew," she says, her voice tentative as she eyes the glass in my hand. "Everything okay?"

The sentiment in her voice is a gut punch, but I do my best to ignore it. If I accept her compassion right now, I'll spiral. "Just a lot on my mind," I say as I gently swirl the brown liquid in my glass, wondering why I poured it to begin with. I quit drinking this shit eleven months ago.

"I'm always here to listen. You know that," she says as the energy in the air shifts. Jace's bulky frame moves towards us, his eyes immediately taking in the whiskey. Without a word, he reaches into the cooler under the bar and pulls out a soda, sliding it over and slipping the still-full tumbler from my fingertips.

friend and Jett's boyfriend, coming from the back and drying his hands with a towel. His eyes slip between me and the glass Jace hasn't emptied yet before settling on my face, studying me.

Noah isn't one of many words. In fact, most of this town thinks he's an irritable grump. Since Jett came into his life at the beginning of this year, he's been much more pleasant, but his demeanor is still questionable at times. And he sees way too damn much. The dude reads people like his girl reads romance novels.

"Noah, cover the counter for a bit, yeah? My bartender should be here any minute."

"Got it, boss," Noah says as he falls into the regular routine of wiping down the bar. He's an elevator mechanic but fills in whenever Jace needs help. Or when the ranch needs an extra hand. Or when Kelsey and Jett need help at the café. You get the point.

If he's asking Noah to cover, it means he's about to drag me out and demand answers. Answers that I don't have. Panicking, I reach forward and snatch the glass from the bar and bring it to my lips.

Before the amber liquid can make contact with my tongue, fingers land on the rim, gently pushing it back to the bar top. Jace's eyes burn a hole through me.

"Bro, what's goin' on?" he asks, his head cocked to the side as he studies me.

"Don't know what you mean." I look around the bar. Anywhere but Jace's questioning gaze seems like a good option. There's no crowd yet, but the regulars will start trickling in within the hour.

"Bullshit," Jace shoots back. "Now, I wouldn't care if you'd come in and asked for a beer. That've been fine. But you quit drinking for a reason, bud, and you know damn well I won't serve you liquor. If this isn't a cry for help, then I don't know what is." He starts to walk toward the back hallway where his office is, motioning me to follow.

"Forget it. It's fine," I mumble as I push off the stool, suddenly too nervous to talk to my best friend about the thoughts suffocating me. Before I can blink, Jace's six-four body is blocking my path, his hand on my shoulder.

"Don't do that man." He shakes his head, messy curls going everywhere. "Don't downplay. You came in for a reason. Let's go talk about it."

I flick my eyes to the door, still halfheartedly thinking about bolting.

Until Jace pulls out his best trick. He knows it, too, by the way he widens his stance, his arms crossing over his massive chest.

"Talk to me, or I call big brother in to get you talking."

I internally groan at the threat of Declan getting involved in more of my shit and grudgingly follow Jace to his office. He stops at the kitchen window and hollers to the cook.

"Hey, Buck. Can you whip together some loaded fries for me? To go?"

"Got it, bossman."

He slaps the counter in thanks and continues down the hall while I follow like the obedient little puppy I am, grumbling all the way.

"Jump off one roof at sixteen, and they baby you for eternity."

Jace turns and gapes at me, his hand twitching. I know he wants to hit me but is scared of hurting my shoulder. The minute I'm one hundred percent cleared is the day Jace Riley lays me out flat.

As he shuts the door behind us, he says, "You know that's not what this is about, man. But if you want to go that route, then what about the motorcycle through the barn door at nineteen? Or the time you tried to go bungee jumping off the roof of the barn that same week? Or how about the time you jumped on that stud colt and nearly died? How about that one, huh?"

Irritation finally snuffs out any of the anxiety I had a moment ago, and I snap. "I get it, okay? I do stupid, reckless shit when I drink. It's why I quit. I just..." I look at Jace, trying to muster the courage to admit this.

I didn't go to the barn this morning expecting to find myself in this situation.

But Jace is my person. My best friend. He's who all of us go to for comfort, for reassurance that we aren't beyond saving. But this? I feel myself ripping apart at the seams.

"Jace..." My voice catches in my throat before I drop onto the couch in here and struggle to take a breath.

Jace's entire demeanor changes, his hand that was tapping out a rhythm on his desk now frozen mid-beat. He leans forward, watching every little movement I make, reading into every breath before saying, "Empty your pockets, brother."

I blanch, the panic setting back in tenfold. "All I did was say your name."

"You've been fiddling with that pocket since we started talking. You came into my bar and poured yourself a drink when you know that shit don't fly with me." He shakes his head, irritation and concern clearly warring with each other. "You just got your struggle with pain pills under control a few months ago. Are you really willing to sit here and lie to me right now?"

I sink deeper into the worn couch cushions, unable to make eye contact. "I haven't taken any. I swear."

Jace expels a harsh breath of relief.

I watch as the gears turn. He's too intelligent to not piece it all together. The silence is deafening, indecision playing in Jace's eyes. I hate the looks of concern and pity that keep flashing across his face.

"You hid them."

"I swear I forgot about them." I hold up my hands defensively. I really did. "Once I found them, I remembered doing it, but I'd just opened the drawer in search of a syringe for a mare on antibiotics. That's it."

"You need to let your brother know."

"No," I snap, shaking my head.

"Yes. Drew, you can't be riding twelve-hundred-pound animals while on that shit, especially when you're not fully cleared as it is."

"I didn't take them, though. We don't need my brother, or worse, Kristen, getting involved. They have enough stress on their plate. Don't add me back to their list."

My brother and his wife, who happens to be the town's only psychologist, have been trying to grow their family but have had issue after issue. They finally decided to quit trying and go the adoption route. Except the excessive amount of red tape is causing even more headache.

Jace sighs again, a sound only I seem to cause, as he paces along the front side of his well-loved computer desk. I think he's had the thing since high school.

I continue before he has time to ask anything. "But I had the pills in my hand."

Faster than I can react, Jace grabs the red and blue stress ball off his desk and chucks it at my good shoulder, hitting his mark with force.

A curse slips out as I rub the injured spot, but I don't say anything else. He's entitled to his frustration. Jace witnessed the development of the issue and my recovery firsthand. After my accident, the doctor had prescribed acetaminophen-oxycodone. The pain was so intense, the damage to my shoulder and back so bad, that I never once questioned taking something stronger than over-the-counter pain killers. Before anyone realized it, my body was hooked. Not long after, so was my mind.

Jace continues staring at me, waiting for me to find the courage to say the rest.

"Just wanted to knock off the edge. I've been restless, like my skin's too tight. Shoulder's been burning again." I almost tell him why I've been restless, but it's been a secret for so long at this point and I don't want to give him another reason to be disappointed in me.

He rakes his hands over his curls and sighs. "Where did you even find any? I thought we went through your apartment and the barn cabinets."

Stopping in front of me with his hand outstretched, he lifts an eyebrow expectantly. "Hand them over."

Without much hesitation—which I'm proud of, by the way—I pull the snack-size baggie from my pocket. Jace quickly removes it from my possession.

"This all of them?" he asks.

I almost nod before guilt immediately sets its claws in me.

He holds his hand out as I reach into my pocket and produce two loose pills. The monster in my mind demands I hold on to them, but I know better than to listen to it.

I've already seen rock bottom. Rather not make a second trip.

Jace places his other hand on my arm in encouragement. "Come on, man."

With a deep, forced breath, I drop the pills into his awaiting hand. Watching him pocket the baggy tightens something in my chest, something I haven't felt in months. Welp, guess that therapy appointment won't be canceled this week. There's too much shit I need to work out, anyway, what with the changes coming our way. Things in Havenwood are about to get a hell of a lot more interesting.

"Why don't you head home. I'll swing by and check in as soon as all my workers get here."

I shake my head but stand and start for the door. "You don't need to. I'll be fine," I lie, knowing I'll fight this feeling well into the morning. Infinite experience with it has proven it won't go away with time.

"Call me if you need me," he concedes, and I know he knows I'm not being honest with either of us. Before I can open the door, he pulls me into an unexpected hug, his massive body engulfing mine.

"Don't make me have to beat your ass," he says, meaning every word. "And grab those fries from the window on your way out."

I nod, emotions too heavy to speak. Sometimes, when you've been friends as long as we have, words aren't needed.

***

Dusk is settling in by the time my boots hit the sidewalk. I slowly make the trek home on foot, the thought of what comes next weighing heavily on me. At least the smell of Buck's loaded chicken fries is a small comfort. Extremely small. Miniscule.

Ah, hell. Nothing can comfort me right now.

Ten months ago, I ruined the best relationship I could ever hope to have. The girl of my dreams, too. Leila Barrett has been through hell and back time and time again, but she always manages to bounce back stronger. More determined. Unstoppable.

And I shattered her heart, tucked tail, and ran back to Georgia like the coward I am.

Two weeks later, I swung my leg over the back of an unbroke stud colt while more than a little inebriated. It ended with emotional trauma for the horse and catastrophic damage to my collarbone and shoulder blade, requiring multiple surgeries, hardware, and physical therapy. A couple hairline spinal fractures luckily healed up on their own. Now my lumbar area twinges with occasional muscle spasms, and stretches are daily routine if I want to use my core muscles.

The last thing on my mind was making amends with the girl whose heart I shattered. She deserved better. She deserves better. But she's moving to Havenwood, back to her home town. Here. And it has me second-guessing every decision I've made since walking out of her hotel room that rainy October day.

I fish keys out of my back pocket while making my way up the winding metal staircase that connects my apartment to the open gym floor. Once inside, I toss the keys and my phone onto the counter then strip my shirt and grab an ice pack from the freezer, gently settling it over my shoulder. The minute I sit in my recliner, a knock sounds at the door.

"Go away!" I yell, already knowing who it is without checking. Should've known better than to trust that Jace wouldn't call Declan the minute I left. The lock flicks a second before the door opens, my brother's annoying face filling the doorframe.

"I locked that for a reason."

"And I unlocked it for a reason, little brother." He closes the door behind him before leaning against it, crossing one dusty brown cowboy boot over the other as he kicks back like he owns the place.

"I need new friends," I grumble halfheartedly. Our brotherhood is still a bit rocky since everything that happened. I blame myself—because I'm the jackass who made stupid choices—but my brother still shoulders some of the guilt for everything that followed his hotel room interruption in Tennessee.

"You have friends who care. That's more than a lot of guys can say."

I push out of my recliner and throwing the icepack haphazardly on the floor in my frustration, storming further into my loft. I'd love to escape his proximity, but my living space is only so big.

"He's worried about you," Declan calls after me. "And quite frankly, so am I."

"I'm fine."

"I'm a married man who knows better than to believe that four letter word, no matter the mouth it comes out of."

That itchy, too-tight feeling is back, squeezing at my chest. I'd love to tell my big brother to shove off, prove to him that I'm a big boy who can handle problems on his own.

But I can't.

I spin away from Declan, my fist connecting with the frame of my bedroom door, wood cracking at the contact. I lean my forehead against the now damaged door, my eyes clenched tight as I try to regain control of my emotions.

"Come on, buddy. You've made it almost six months. Don't throw that away."

Feeling sick—and hating myself more than a little—I rip the pill from my pocket and step into the bathroom, immediately flushing it down the toilet before melting to the floor, my back against the wall. My breaths are shaky, all energy gone. I lean my head back against the gray-tiled wall as Declan sits beside me.

"I wasn't going to take it," I whisper after a few tense moments of silence.

"Glad to hear it. You wanna talk about why you kept it, then?" he asks just as softly. Before my head even moves, he's jumping in. "If you aren't gonna talk to me, talk to Kristen."

A mix of anxiety, irritation, and guilt swirls in my gut. Another instance of small-town life coming to bite me in the ass since his wife is the only mental health professional within a thirty-mile radius.

I scoff, turning my focus to folding the clothes on my bed instead of watching my brother study me. I'm tired of everyone looking so closely. Always looking for the weakest point to poke and prod to see if I'll fall again. "Watch out, the addict might crumble under pressure."

I can see Declan nod in my periphery, and it causes heat to creep up my neck at the embarrassment of it all. The sarcasm clearly didn't take.

"You know as well as anyone what this is, Drew. You're struggling with Leila coming back to town, with what that means for the both of you." He continues to stare as I put my clothes away, my attempt at ignoring him not phasing him in the slightest. Then he hits me where it hurts, his words nearly collapsing me on the spot. "I know there's still at least one pain pill in your pocket, kid."

My entire body freezes, air wheezing from my lungs. "You're out of your mind," I choke out.

"Don't bullshit a bullshitter."

He and I lock into a stare down, the same dark-blue eyes staring back at each other, neither brother speaking for a time. I don't know what he sees in my expression, but Declan's eyes finally soften.

"Empty your pockets, bro. Prove me wrong."

"Declan, no. I'm not talking to your wife about this."

"Either talk to her, talk to me, or we talk to mom and dad together."

"That's messed up."

"So is hiding pills."

I shake my head, running calloused fingers through my mess of black hair. "Mom doesn't need the worry, and Dad can't know. He'd pull me from the training rides, and I need the saddle time. Please." I'm not above begging. I'd drop to my knees if I wasn't already on the bathroom floor.

I can't lose the extra rides, the freedom. I just got back in the saddle a month ago and am still dealing with limitations and lack of strength in core areas. I need both the adrenaline high and the mental stillness those four-legged creatures provide.

Declan sighs. "Okay, Kristen said she'll be waiting on you first thing tomorrow."

Incredulous, I stare at him. "You already talked to her."

He nods, unashamed.

I curse.

"She was with me when Jace called. But that brings me to why I was already on my way out the door to talk to you. Now, though, I'm questioning if I should even tell you."

"What, it wasn't just a wellness check?" I joke, but the humor falls flat as I take in my brother's expression. "What, man?"

"Did Leila ever contact you?"

I shrug. "She left a voicemail or two. A text here and there. I never listened to them. Why?"

He stares at me, and I think I'm going to have to press him for the information, but the look he gives me halts me in my tracks.

"Leila and Gavin came in a day early. Along with her seven-week-old daughter. *Your* daughter, Drew."

Chapter 3
Leila

Five in the morning is peaceful in Havenwood.

No cars on the street rushing to beat big city traffic. No noise except that of nature.

It's soothing.

Unless you have an angry newborn with the lungs of a mandrake. Since she isn't in her usual bassinette with the blackout curtains and extra loud sound machine, she has woken up every hour or so. My nipples ache from the constant cluster feeds, my temples pound with the building stress and lack of sleep, and I probably look like a racoon at this point.

my feet into my running shoes, grab some cash, and slip out as quietly as I can. Hopefully the coffee shop is open.

***

Gavin's old house, the one we just moved back into, sits on the outskirts of town. And although Havenwood is tiny with less than 2,500 people, it contains a lot of land. It means my early morning run to the town square is roughly three miles. Since it's a Saturday, there's nearly zero traffic and the roads are quiet as I jog along the sidewalks.

When I found out that I was pregnant with Kaia, I had to make a choice: stay on my anti-depressants and anxiety meds with unknown risks to baby or quit taking them. Running and punching things seem to be the only outlets that have helped me. I jogged daily until thirty-two weeks and was finally able to start back a week ago. It's a lot of stop and go as I regain that part of myself. And now that I've been lucky enough to breastfeed, I've been too worried about trying to balance a new medication on top of everything else.

As I make it to the outskirts of the square, everything is still quiet. The only thing open is the old café, which has had a major renovation since the last time I was here. Granted, that was a decade ago, but the old sign has been replaced with one that says *The Write Brew*. It's beautiful inside, the olive green popping with the soft lavender and dark wood floors and counters. I'm still taking in the new bookstore side when a squeal pierces my ear right before I'm tackled in a hug.

Kelsey Riley's tiny frame wraps around me like a spider monkey.

"I can't believe you guys are actually here!" She glances around, as if expecting someone to be walking in behind me. Like anyone else is mentally unstable enough to join me on a pre-dawn run. "Is Kaia with Gavin?" she asks in a near-whisper.

I just nod, still not sure how to react to being in her presence again. My brother's best friend has always been a spitfire. She's impossible not to like, making friends with everyone she meets. She's the only person Gavin shared things with while I was pregnant, although she doesn't know who the father is. Gavin swore to leave that to me, and until yesterday when Declan showed up to help us unpack and just immediately knew Kaia was his niece, I was waiting to tell anyone else until Drew knew.

"Kaia was having a rough go of being in a new place, so Gavin is at the house snuggling her while I went for a run. Needed to clear my head a bit."

She starts walking toward the counter and gestures to it. "Coffee, pastries, or both?" I'm about to pull a fresh pan of blueberry scones out from the back. They have the most amazing sugar glaze drizzled on top."

I give her a knowing look. "You licked the bowl, didn't you?"

"Hell yes I did, missy. I know better than to let the tasty things in life go to waste."

She sets about fixing two coffees and some pastries before stepping into the back and returning with two scones. She never once asks what I want, just preps it all and sets it in a big bag with handles. "I'll give you a ride back home."

"Oh, you don't need to do that."

"It's three miles. You're not walking that far back while carrying my delicious treats. They're too precious to eat cold. Now, let's go." She hollers to the back area, "Hey, Jett. Wakey, wakey. I'll be back soon."

A faint "nighty-night" sounds from the back room.

Kelsey grins to herself. "Jett is my co-owner. She runs the book side of things but is really good at the coffee side, too."

"Is she actually awake?"

Kelsey flips her hand in dismissal. "That girl can nearly match my energy at the drop of a hat. She'll be on it if anyone decides to venture in before I get back. But honestly, with it being Saturday, the likelihood of anyone coming in this early is slim."

We walk out front, and Kelsey leads me to her car, setting the bag of goods in the back seat.

"Run into anyone yet?" she asks with a sideways glance, and I immediately know she's referring to Drew.

I shake my head. "Declan was there when we came in, but this is my first time venturing out. Hell of a time of day to explore, right?" I push a strand of loose hair from my face. "This is good, though," I say with much more confidence than I feel. "I wanted to lay eyes on the town, see what's what without anyone breathing down my neck. I haven't been back since I was sixteen. Now, I'm here with a kid in tow. There's bound to be gossip."

She laughs, the trill soft in the silence of her car. "Well, yeah. It's Havenwood. We take care of our own, and you, my dear friend, are about to be bombarded with people wanting to help you guys settle in."

That's what I'm worried about. This town has a way of making you look deep into things you'd rather forget. Even if they all mean well.

every week over video chat. I'm doing this, whether you want to be a part of it or not. You know how to reach me.

And now she's here. *They* are here.

Leila told me, but I was too focused on my own pain to read a single text message—and there's a ton of those, too, now that I'm scrolling through them. Even though she never heard from me, she still sent screenshots of ultrasounds and updates. She never quit trying to reach out.

How the hell am I supposed to face them after I abandoned them?

***

"About time you showed up," Jace chirps as I step off the last stair into the gym. The dude must have been a golden retriever in a past life. He's always too happy-go-lucky, even at five thirty in the morning. Although I know he feels it, the only visible sign of his concern is the flick of his eyes to the back brace around my waist before he makes eye contact again.

"Don't know why I agreed to this. Did you even go to sleep?" I ask as I begin bouncing on the balls of my feet, trying to get blood flowing and the bone-deep tiredness pushed out. Bypassing his offered roll of tape, I slip my hands into my quick wraps.

"Did you?" he shoots back before stepping up to the heavyweight bag hanging in the corner of the room and starting a sequence of one-two combinations.

I step in to hold the bag steady as his hits increase in force. "Not a lick. Watch your knee on the follow-through."

He pauses long enough to adjust his feet and reangle his body before returning to his left jab–right cross pattern, adding in the occasional left hook as his muscles loosen.

After a few minutes, he backs away, still bouncing on his toes. "Swap me."

I start with the same pattern but with a fraction of his power. I've only been cleared for physical workouts for a month, and the muscles are slow to rebuild. I'm not anywhere close to peak fitness yet. I continue with the combination sequence, noting the stiffness throughout my core as I rotate through a punch.

"You're tight today."

My noncommittal grunt gives him the hint that I don't want to talk. He knows it. It's the same sound he's heard for the nearly thirty years of our friendship. And yet, he still pushes.

"Not in the mood for *that's what she said* comebacks, I take it. Okay, how about this? The word on the street is the Barretts moved back yesterday. Did you know? Kelsey was ecstatic when Gavin called last night. How long you think until they finally tie the knot?"

I swing harder than intended on the added left hook and let out a curse as it sets fire to my shoulder. The broken bones may have healed thanks to hardware, but the tendons and ligaments haven't been as kind. Jace immediately tunes in to my reaction, slipping into the caretaker role he's been known for our entire lives.

Maybe he's more Anatolian shepherd than retriever.

"You need to take a break, man?" he asks, already stepping toward the cooler in the corner.

Instead of answering, I ask another question. "What else did Kelsey say?"

He shrugs. "Not much. We may be twins, but she's loyal to a fault and hasn't shared any details of why they're back." Pulling an ice pack from the cooler, he tosses it to me before stepping back up to the bag. "Besides, figured you'd know more."

I try to school my features even though shock courses through my body. He can't know, can he? I made certain never to mention our time together, but there's no telling what might have been said when I was recovering. Many of those days and weeks were a blur.

"What do you mean?"

"Dec is still friends with Gavin, yeah? I just assumed he'd have told you more. Besides"—he grins— "we all figured you and little Leila Barrett would end up married and raising the next generation of colt breakers and cowgirls taking over the ranch."

I huff a laugh, even though this conversation is far from humorous.

His words? That was the plan.

I had it all worked out. Where we'd live. How I'd propose. What she'd look like in a simple white dress with our friends and family surrounding us.

Now, I'll be lucky if Gavin Barrett doesn't kill me on sight for what I did to his little sister.

I undo the Velcro of my brace then sling it over the stair railing before grabbing a towel and wiping my face and neck as I settle onto one of the benches. Luckily, no one else in town is stupid enough to hit the gym at this hour on the weekend.

I take a deep breath. "Remember those trips to Tennessee I was making with Declan?"

"Yeah, that last one is when shit hit the fan between you two."

"I wasn't going for ranch reasons. The guys up there can easily load horses for him. I was making up bullshit excuses to tag along because he always met up with Gavin at least once while we were there."

I can almost hear the gears turning in Jace's mind as he pieces it all together.

them. No need to when I've walked past them a thousand times.

My petite, blonde-headed sister-in-law sits in a black swivel chair behind her oversize desk, feet kicked up and inadvertently showcasing her flamingo socks.

"Nice feet."

Kristen jumps, those bright-pink flamingos quickly finding the floor. "Make noise, boy," she says while brushing her hair out of her startlingly pale blue eyes. "About time you showed up, though. I was starting to think you'd flake out on me."

Instinctively, my body tenses, going on the defensive.

"I'm fine, Kris," I snap, tempted to turn around and leave, my brother's threat be damned.

"I have roughly forty-five minutes before my first session. Come sit with me," she says as she stands and walks to the picture window, taking a seat on the couch and crossing her feet underneath herself.

"I don't need you to pick my brain."

She lifts a brow. "Then why are you here?" When I don't answer, she continues. "I'm not your therapist, and you aren't my client. But you are my little brother for all intents and purposes. I just want to know where your head is and see if I can help."

I fist and release my hands a few times, letting the short nails dig into my palms and relishing the bite as the fight slowly seeps from my muscles. I join Kristen on the couch. She sits quietly, letting me wrap my head around what I want to say.

"Where's Hope?" I ask, referring to Kristen's therapy dog. I could really go for some puppy snuggles.

"Declan took her to the barn today. She's been getting into things at the house, so we decided to let her burn off some energy out there instead."

Damn. I roll my shoulders, trying to exude the confidence that I definitely do not feel. "I can't afford to do it again."

"Do what?"

I cut my eyes at her. "Don't act clueless, Kristen. It's not a good look for you. I know my brother ran his mouth."

A fire lights in her glacier-blue eyes at the slight toward her husband. Awesome. I'm pushing buttons without even meaning to, today. "Your brother may have a big mouth, but his heart is even bigger. He doesn't know any more than what he saw. And you don't have to talk to me about it if you don't want to."

I squeeze my eyes closed, my knee bouncing with nervous energy. After a few cleansing breaths, I open my eyes and exhale slowly. My gut says she already knows, but I need to judge her reaction for myself, to know that the people I love and trust purposely kept me in the dark.

"I have a daughter, and none of you bothered to tell me."

"Your brother didn't know she was yours until yesterday."

I scoff, arms crossing over my chest as I look away.

"And I couldn't have told you without violating—"

"—patient confidentiality. Yeah, yeah." Groaning, I push up and walk to the window, staring out at the barn. It's tough to see from here, but I can just barely make out a few of the horses in the paddock by the arena. That's where I'd rather be right now.

"I will admit to yesterday being a new low for me," I finally say, eyes still trained outside. "I haven't felt this pathetic in a long time. It shook me pretty good—all of it—but I'm tough."

"Tough enough to handle Leila and a baby on your own, right?"

Shit.

"You can't rush over there and bombard her with questions. You can't demand she let you see a daughter you've never met."

A terrifying thought crosses my mind. "How much does she know?"

Kristen's eyes soften as she studies me, taking in my question.

"How much does she know, Kristen?"

"She knows everything."

***

The old red barn is my favorite place in Havenwood. Hell, maybe in the whole world. I've never been farther than the Savannah coastline or the Blue Ridge mountains, so I wouldn't really know.

With it being August, most of the horses are in their stalls under fans and quietly munching on hay. I slip down to the last stall on the right. It's the largest one we have—three stalls opened into one—for the horse I ruined.

If anyone needs proof that I don't deserve a chance with my daughter or a second chance with Leila, this little gelding is it. The sign on his stall warning everyone not to enter, the paddock entrance added to the backside of his stall.

But for some insane reason, the only human he wants near him is me. The asshat who tried to prove a point and failed. I cannot, in fact, break a colt while intoxicated. A stupid decision led to a freak accident that resulted in my broken body and his broken mind.

Stepping up to the stall and opening the hay door, I give a gentle click before whispering, "Hey, big guy."

He takes a tentative step toward me. Then another until his nose rests against my open palm. He lips the skin before blowing into my hand.

I chuckle, reaching into my back pocket for the soft peppermint Havoc is searching for. He grumbles greedily as I undo the wrapper and present it to him.

Chapter 6
Leila

"Hey, Gav? Where did you put the bouncer?" I ask, sticking my head into the living room. We've been trying to unpack for three days. I didn't think we brought this much with us, but it feels like a never-ending battle.

"Pretty sure it's in the nursery."

"Pretty sure it's not," I shoot back.

The doorbell rings as I turn to check the nursery for the third time. Right on time, Kaia lets out a cry from where she was napping in my room.

I feel like crying, too, baby.

Gavin pops around the corner, already on his way to Kaia. "The kid from the grocery store said he'd just leave it on the porch. Sorry."

I rub at my forehead, stress and lack of sleep triggering yet another headache. "It's fine. I'll go check."

Hopefully, he'll be able to get Kaia back down. She's only been asleep for about a half hour, and this mama needs a break from the cluster feeds that still haven't eased.

I sling the door open, ready to chew out the delivery guy for not reading the drop-off instructions, but then I freeze.

Oh so slowly, my gaze travels from the worn-out cowboy boots to the stacked and broken-in jeans. The gray V-neck that stretches tight over a well-muscled chest. Black ink peeking out of both sleeves, the intricate designs I used to know intimately.

I study the light stubble on his jaw, not letting my eyes travel any higher. If I don't look up, maybe he'll disappear.

"Hey, Leila Grace."

So much for going *poof*.

Every possible emotion flows through me at the sound of my name on his lips.

Anxiety. Fear. Exuberance.

Hope.

Gavin's footsteps and Kaia's fussy whimpers sound behind me. "Was it the groceries? I think she wants another feed. She's trying to eat me through my shirt. Doesn't believe me when I tell her she won't get any of the good stuff by latching on to cotton."

I finally force my eyes to meet the man who walked away without a second glance. The one who has had my heart in his ironclad grip since I was ten years old. The one who promised me forever.

Drew Flynn.

Andrew Malakai Flynn, to be specific.

"Not groceries," I finally choke out, although I know Gavin is close enough to see that for himself.

The fear and anxiety I'm feeling? It looks like it's about tenfold on Drew's face as he takes in Kaia's tiny body against Gavin's broad chest.

"Had an errand to run for Dad and was hoping...is that..." he trails off, his expression shifting to one of awe. It's enough to kick my brain back into gear.

Grabbing Drew's hand and pulling him inside so I can shut the door to the heat, I gently take Kaia from Gavin and promptly place her in Drew's unexpecting arms.

"You woke her with the doorbell. You get to hold her while I prep her bottle." I do at least make sure he has her cradled against himself, and when I say he looks good holding a baby? Our daughter? I think my ovaries just cried for another.

I hear Gavin guiding Drew to the living room and helping him settle on the couch. Should I have pushed her on him that quickly? Probably not. But I've played this scenario out multiple times every day for the last forty-plus weeks, and none of those times were smooth sailing.

It's wild. Even through the heartache of losing whatever connection we had, I always knew Drew would be a great dad. He can handle anything, just like my dad always did.

Quickly pulling out one of the bottles I pumped earlier and setting it under the hot running water of the sink, I peek around the opening of the living room. Drew is a natural, just like I knew he'd be. He has Kaia curled against his chest as he gently bounces in place, bobbing a pacifier against her gums with his free hand as a distraction. It's working for the moment.

By the time the bottle is warm and I step back into the living room, Drew's face has morphed into one of pure adoration. Exactly what I'd known—what I'd hoped deep down, anyway—would happen when he held Kaia for the first time. I step forward and offer him the bottle, and that flash of fear that I see on my own face every day when I look in the mirror appears on Drew's.

"I haven't bottle fed anything more than a calf a few years ago."

Gavin coughs to hide his laugh, but the crinkles around his eyes give him away.

Chapter 7
Drew

After feeding and burping my daughter for the first time, I left a sleeping Kaia and Leila with the promise of a serious conversation in the near future. At the time, I'd meant for the conversation to happen that evening. Instead, we've been bouncing around each other for two days. I stop by before heading to the barn, but it's usually just long enough for Leila to grab a shower while I snuggle Kaia.

Best damn thirty minutes of my day.

But today is the day we finally sit down and figure out what the future—our future—looks like. As soon as I get some horses ridden.

As I walk into the aisle of the poorly lit sale barn, Declan slings a saddle over a young filly's back. For a mare, she's easy going and willing. The kind of mount I'm stuck with for now.

"You wanna take this one out?" Declan asks without looking up from doing up the cinch. He checks the saddle once more before patting her on the neck and turning to me.

I step past the horse and my brother, grabbing the work bridle before unclipping the crossties and sliding the bridle over her halter.

Declan stands in my way, forcing me to look up the few inches into his face. "You good?"

I roll my eyes. "You going to ask me that every time you see me?"

"For a while, yeah." He steps to the side, letting me and the mare move toward the arena.

I walk past without another word, my brain already in ride mode.

I was born to be in the saddle. Never once have I questioned that. It requires awareness of every breath, every turn of the head, every shift of the hips. The fact that a thousand-pound animal can be that reactive, that in tune to the human on its back, never ceases to fascinate me.

After I throw a leg over, I take a moment to lower myself into the saddle and breathe, letting the mare feel me relax. No rush. No worries. Just me and her and nature.

I could've lost it all. Everything I've worked for should have gone up in flames.

I still hear the crunch of my shoulder against the metal panel of the round pen. I still have nightmares where I grip the horn as Havoc goes down on our left side, the pain or the concussion or both knocking me out.

I'm lucky. I'm lucky to be here. I'm lucky Leila wants me in Kaia's life. I'm lucky our daughter is too young to realize how much of a mess I am.

As I work the little mare in and out of circles, encouraging to find her own balance, my mind drifts to the little human I held in my arms earlier. The tiny fingers that grasped mine and wouldn't let go. The way Leila still soothes my nerves, even while staying out of reach. The way my heart still pounds at just the sight of her. She's still the most beautiful girl I've ever known, inside and out.

I step the filly into a slow-legged canter, letting her stretch her neck, her long black mane catching the wind as she moves. As we turn the corner near the barn, Declan steps up to the fence. I pull up the mare, but her brakes are sharper than I expect. My left hand pushes into the horn, jarring my shoulder. I wince enough for Declan to notice, concern filling his features.

"If you keep getting hurt, I'm not going to ready these guys for you anymore."

I chuckle as I rotate the shoulder a few times, trying to work out the twinge I now feel. "I'd just get them ready myself. What's a little more damage from slinging saddles?"

"Not funny." He shakes his head in disbelief, or maybe in total belief. He knows how stubborn I am. "Gavin just called. Said he wanted to talk if you had time."

I pat my back pocket, realizing I must have left my phone in the barn. "How long have I been out here?"

"About an hour."

I reach a hand down to scratch the mare on her withers, whispering encouragement and praise before slinging my leg over and dismounting. "Such a good girl," I murmur while letting her scratch against me until a farmhand steps up and takes the reins from me to untack and hose her down.

"I can literally feel you worrying, Dec," I say as I rake my hand through sweat-soaked hair.

"Are you sure you aren't jumping too fast here?"

"You mean with Leila? It's not like I'm jumping into bed with her."

"You already did that, didn't you?" he asks wryly.

I grip the ends of my hair, frustration pouring out of me on a groan. "That wasn't fair," I finally say. "You know damn well that I'm in love with that girl. I have been since I was twelve years old. And I am going to regret the last year until the day that I die. But you do not get to throw my daughter in my face."

He opens his mouth, probably to try to smooth over his words, but I cut him off. It's been long enough. I've kept my feelings from that time to myself for long enough. Looking my brother dead in the eye, I tell him the truth of what happened after he walked in on us.

"I was going to drive back up that next weekend. I'd already cleared it with Dad. Told him why and everything. Then she texted me. Said she needed to figure things out on her own for a bit. To give her some time to tell Gavin about us. She didn't know I'd already talked to him. Asked for his blessing the same day I bought the ring." I huff a laugh, but it's filled with so much pain at the memories that surge forward that it comes out choked. "Then the fiasco with Havoc happened, the surgeries, everything. She called, texted, left messages. I ignored them all, because I knew I wasn't good enough for her. Didn't listen to them until the other day."

"Drew." It's not often my brother's voice cracks with emotion. I can read the apology on his face, but it isn't good enough.

"No. You weren't supportive when you found us together back in October. You're being a dick about things right now. I will do my job to the best of my ability, but my personal life and choices are not your concern. And if you know what's good for you, you'll keep your mouth shut around my daughter and the mother of my child." I start the walk into town, calling over my shoulder, "I'll take the other mare for a spin when it cools off this evening."

No footsteps follow me. No voices holler after me. It hurts more than it should.

***

It's more than a little tempting to head over to Riley's Bar and Grill, but I'm unprepared to handle any heart-to-heart conversations with Jace after the way today has gone. Instead, I cut across the town square to slip inside The Write Brew. Maybe Kelsey can slip me one of her "off-the-record" frilly coffee drinks. Don't judge. They taste like coffee milkshakes when she makes them.

Instead of a sugar rush, an unexpected scolding cuts me off before I can decide if I want caramel or chocolate or both.

"Andrew Malakai Flynn, how dare you."

I freeze, the sound of my mother's voice locking me in place. "I don't even have the door to The Write Brew all the way open yet, and I'm already getting full named?"

"Don't you talk back to your mama, boy," she scolds with a smack to the back of my head. It's then that I take in who else is in the little café. Kelsey and Jett are at one of the couches on the bookstore side, a tiny bundle tucked into Jett's chest.

Uh-oh.

"You have some explaining to do," Mama whispers. Her eyes are shining with joy, but there's too many questions in that gaze.

I wrap my mom into a tight hug, praying she doesn't disown me for not filling her in on everything from the last few days. Months?

I'm severely lacking in what the protocol is for telling your mother that you had a secret relationship that resulted in a baby and then you unknowingly abandoned baby and mother because you were too selfish to listen to messages.

Yeah, that sounds like a perfect thing to tell the most nurturing human being to grace this Earth.

I slip away from her and walk over to Jett, silently begging her to pass my daughter to me. In true Jett fashion, she sticks her tongue out at me but ultimately hands over Kaia after making me use the hand sanitizer on the table next to her.

I bounce gently with Kaia curled into my arm. It's still terrifying to hold such a small, fragile being, but I'm getting more comfortable with it.

Kaia's eyes are so blue. I can't help but wonder if she'll end up with my eyes or if they'll turn as she gets older. Studying her face, I step closer to my mom.

"Mama, I'd like you to officially meet Kaia. Your granddaughter."

Her eyes mist over as she tentatively reaches a hand out to squeeze Kaia's bootie-covered toes. "I expect you three over for dinner tomorrow night."

"I don't know if Leila would be up for—"

"Not up for discussion. Family dinner. Tell Gavin to tag along as well if he'd like. I want *all* my babies under my roof for a meal."

"Yes, ma'am." I glance to Kelsey. "Where is she, anyway?" I ask, gesturing to Kaia. "More than a little surprised to find my daughter without her or Gavin."

Kelsey returns from behind the counter, a sugary concoction in hand. "Leila had an appointment and Gavin needed to run some errands. I volun-told them to leave Kaia with me," she says as she passes me the drink.

I nod my thanks as I shift Kaia in my arms to take a sip. Knowing how stubborn both Barrett siblings are, I ask, "How'd that go over?"

"'Bout as well as you'd think. But they both need a break." Her eyes soften as she gives me a pointed look. "You guys need to figure something out. She's running on fumes, D."

I nod, looking away to avoid the guilt that hasn't stopped eating at me. "Working on it," I mumble before stepping back to my mother and letting her coo over her first grandchild while a plan starts to spin in my head. It'll take some work and some major convincing, but it just might be doable.

Chapter 8
Leila

Therapy sucks. Sometimes, I wonder if it wouldn't be easier to just let the memories lie where they are and quit digging into the bad parts. My emotions are all over the place. First, I had a nightmare but instead of the usual terrors playing back like memories, it was of something happening to Kaia. When I finally gave up on sleep, I fell apart in the kitchen because there weren't any little spoons in the drawer when I wanted to eat cereal.

It's stupid. A grown-ass woman should not overreact because the only spoon available is a big one. And yet, here I am hours later and still irritated about it.

Kristen says it's probably a combination of my usual bad thoughts mixing with postpartum rise and fall. It's been a day. Jett and Kelsey have Kaia. It gives me the good kind of chills to realize that we actually have a support system here, more than just Gavin.

Taking advantage of the fact that I have a few hours to myself without feeling guilty for pawning my daughter off on Gavin,

I start the walk to the ranch. It's been too long since I've felt a horse's mane under my fingers. Even longer since I've been in the saddle. Maybe I can talk Drew into a trail ride one of these days.

I wander down the barn aisle, glancing at each horse that is in for the day. Most of them are too busy munching on alfalfa to notice the human ogling over them. As I make it to the end of the barn, I come up on an oversize stall. A stocky built, leggy chestnut stands with his head in the corner, but his ears twitch as I approach. His feet stay planted, nose to hay, but he knows I'm here. He's watching. Calculating.

A sign on his stall reads *Weary of Humans. Keep Out.* I chuff a laugh.

"You and me both, buddy," I whisper as I lean against the stall door and glance out the end of the barn, taking in the breathtaking views of the rolling green pastures, the scent of horses a long-forgotten comfort.

A soft snort and sniff at my shoulder makes me glance back into the stall. The chestnut has come out of the corner, now leaning his nose against the stall bars. I run my knuckles gently along his muzzle, the bruised skin from the bag work in my morning workout protesting at the contact. Even still, I continue scratching the gelding's nose all the way up to the cowlicks between his eyes as we soak up each other's company.

A time later, though I'm unsure if it was ten minutes or an hour, the air stirs behind me about the same time the gelding's ears flick back. I turn my head, hand pausing mid-stroke, to find Drew standing against the stall across from us.

"Wondered how long it'd take for you two to realize you weren't alone anymore."

"What's with the warning sign?" I ask immediately. "This guy's a sweetheart."

I'm surprised to find Drew hesitating in his answer. "He's the horse I was on when we went down."

My eyebrows shoot up. "This is the horse Gav said shoulda been put down?"

Drew nods. "When Declan realized the extent of the trauma to this guy's mind, he started questioning if it was something that could be overcome. Being the phenomenal horseman that he is, though, he gave Havoc the time and space he needed. Moved him to one of the big back fields with a few of the old retired geldings where he wouldn't be around people or vehicles."

"Then I'm assuming you started building trust with him as soon as you could."

He nods. "As soon as I was back on two feet, I started spending a few hours a day just sitting by the round bales reading or listening to music."

"Seems like he bounced back."

"He's still extremely skittish in the arena. He'll probably never accept a saddle thanks to me, but he'll never live a day not spoiled like a little pasture princess."

"You're a good man, Drew. A good horseman. Anyone who's met you knows that."

He shrugs one shoulder.

"You'll be a good father, too. I wouldn't have come back if I didn't know it deep in my bones."

"As long as you're good with me having absolutely zero clue on how to do this."

I nod.

"I know you said you aren't interested in *us*, but I'd like to take you to dinner tonight—you and Kaia—and let you get reacquainted with everyone."

"Who is everyone?" I ask hesitantly. The idea of being around crowds after not having a social life for so long creates a mix of excitement and nerves.

"Kelsey and Jace. I guess you've already met Jett, but my buddy Noah will be there, too. Reece may duck in, but you're more likely to see him out here somewhere. He's Dec's right hand and Jett's older brother."

"Gotta warn you, my moods haven't been the best lately. Not sure I'll be good company."

"Well, we need to talk anyway. So, what do you say we do that now, then swing back by to grab Kaia before getting together with everyone. Then I can talk you into the family dinner that my mom demands we all attend tomorrow night."

"Um, excuse me. What?" I probably look like a deer caught in headlights, but I can't have heard him correctly.

He nods. "Yeah, funny story. She was at the café earlier, met Kaia, and said we all better be at her house tomorrow night to eat. Not sure about you, but I'm not a fan of telling that woman no."

My gut reaction is to tell him no, consequences be damned. Not because I don't want his parents to spend time with their granddaughter, but because that house was always a safe space for me. Mr. and Mrs. Flynn were like a second set of parents after I lost my dad and got stuck with the woman who birthed me. They made sure I was clean, full, and aware that their door was always open. My reaction to say no stems from the fear of seeing the disappointment etched on their faces.

Because what could be more disappointing than disappearing for ten years without so much as a phone call?

Turning up with their son's secret love child. That's what.

"Where's your head at, sunshine?"

"In the clouds where it belongs," I mumble without thinking. The little smirk on his face is the first clue that I'm busted. "No fair. You did that on purpose."

He shrugs. "Wanted to see if it was still your reflexive answer."

"Duh. Of course it is. Has been since we were kids."

He takes a step forward, hand reaching hesitantly. His fingers graze mine but don't take hold. "Seriously, Leila Grace. Where's your head?" The look in his midnight eyes has me wanting to melt, to go back to how things were and bare my soul to the man in front of me. To let him take care of me, wash away every bad thought.

But I can't. I refuse to be weak. I'm here for our daughter. Not for me. The love we had for each other is gone, irreparable.

Taking a step back, I pull myself together. Drew's lips turn down at the move, but he doesn't call me out on it.

"I'm sure your mother is disappointed in me," I finally mumble, looking anywhere but at him.

"My mother loves and misses you. She's irritated with me for not being there, but she has zero ill will toward you. She still thinks of you as her daughter," he says, slipping his hands into his pockets and leaning against the stall, one boot crossed over the other.

Why is that so attractive?

"I'll get on my knees and beg if that's what it takes, sunshine."

I sigh as I shake my head. "Will there at least be banana pudding?"

The grin that takes over Drew's face is infinitely more dangerous than anything else in my life right now. He looks every bit the cowboy he is but without the stress and turmoil of the last year.

Is it wrong that I want to keep that look on his face?

"Banana pudding and groveling will be added to the menu. I'll make sure of it."

"Now, wait just a minute. I didn't say anything about groveling."

"No, but it's necessary. I have my work cut out for me, but I'm willing to find out where this goes. Are you?"

Am I? Or am I already getting in way over my head with a certain blue-eyed boy who still makes my heart go boom?

Chapter 9
Leila

By the time I get back to Kaia, it's been hours, the longest I've been away since she was born, and the pure need to have her back in my arms can't be described. I probably look like a madwoman holding a newborn hostage with how tightly I have her wrapped against my chest, but I don't care. Risking a glance up at Kelsey and Drew, I sigh in relief when there isn't judgment on their faces.

"She was good?" I ask Kelsey, hoping Kaia wasn't too fussy for her.

"Slept like an angel," she says with a smile. "Auntie Kelsey will keep her any time you need. I think Jett liked having her around, too."

Drew snorts. "She had Kaia tucked pretty close when I was in here earlier. Safe to say she may end up with baby fever."

"Noah would be thrilled, but Jett's more the 'borrow and return' type. She likes her freedom."

I huff. "Yeah, she definitely doesn't want a little one, then. I wouldn't trade this one for the world, but I haven't slept more than two hours at a time since the first trimester. And today's the first time I've left her for more than an hour or two."

I try to ignore the look of concern on Drew's face as he takes in my statement. It's true, though. Sleep doesn't come easily for me. Between the nightmares, paranoia that something will happen to Kaia while I sleep, and her eating every two or three hours, REM sleep doesn't exist in my life.

"I'll leave the play pen up in the office, so she's free to come play whenever you need a break," she says as she wraps her arms around me in a hug, careful not to jostle Kaia.

"Love you, Kels," I whisper tearfully.

"Our brave girl," she whispers back. "Try to trust him, yeah?"

I nod into her shoulder, knowing she means Drew.

As I strap Kaia into her infant carrier, Drew gathers her bag and blanket before slipping the carrier from my hands as well.

"I can carry her," I say, but it sounds much poutier than I meant for it to.

"I know," he says before starting for the door.

I glance at Kelsey for help, but she just grins. "Let him help. You know he's a good man, through and through. He already loves that little girl. You should've seen him showing her off to his mama and anyone else who came through that door earlier."

A soft smile lifts my lips, but I can't help the caution I still feel in my gut. "I've never questioned if he'd be a good father or not. Kaia will always have his heart."

It's mine I'm worried about.

When I get to Drew's truck, I can't stop the giggle that slips out. He's staring at the seatbelt like it's a snake about to strike as he tries to strap in the carrier.

"Need some help?" I ask.

He jumps, smacking his ballcap-covered head against the truck roof.

I wince in sympathy. "Are you okay?"

"How the hell does this thing strap in? It can't be as complicated as I'm making it."

I grip his hip while gently pushing him out of the way, my fingers *not* lingering once he shifts to the side, before I quickly buckle the carrier into the middle seat. "It's easier in Gavin's vehicle. We just have a base that it clicks into."

"Can you send me the link? I'll get one that can stay in the truck."

I keep my face turned away so he can't see the effect of his words. I'm melting for this man all over, and it is terrifying.

"Leila," Drew rumbles, breaking me from my thoughts.

"Hmm?"

"You're spacing. All good?"

"Oh. Yeah. Just finding some of this more challenging than I expected."

"If this is about the car seat, I'm sorry if I overstepped—"

"No. It's a good idea. A great one, really. My hormones just have my emotions all over the place." Staring out the window as we drive the few miles down to Gavin's, I try to sort through my thoughts. "I think it was relief. You just rolled with it."

As we pull into the drive, Drew puts the truck in park and turns to me, taking my hands in his. "I'm in, Leila. As much in as you'll let me be."

The conversation pauses as Drew unbuckles Kaia's carrier and loops his arm through the handle before grabbing her bag and walking up the drive to the front porch. I'm slow to get out of the truck, my gaze stuck on the sight before me.

From his hat to his boots and a baby on his arm, the man is sexy. He doesn't even struggle with the awkward weight of the carrier, but it's probably lighter than the hay bales he's used to slinging. Shirtless and sweaty. Muscles rippling as he goes.

Reel it in, Leila Grace. *Sheesh.*

Quickening my steps, I slip in front of Drew and open the front door.

"You can set her carrier in the living room. I'm gonna change really quick."

I snag the first shirt I find and swap it with the sweat-soaked one I'm wearing. This damn humidity is killing me. So are my boobs. By the time I slip back into the living room to convince Kaia to eat, Drew is on the couch with her cuddled into his chest, her little blue eyes blinking up at him. He's just as enraptured by her.

"Hate to interrupt the bonding time, but I need to nurse her."

He startles. "Oh, yeah." He shifts forward to ease the transition.

"It won't bother you if I feed her out here, will it?"

"Don't worry about me, Leila. You do what you need to."

"Just making sure. Don't want to make you uncomfortable."

He stretches tall, studying me like he's ready to take on the world. "Has someone made you feel guilty for feeding our daughter?"

"Well, no," I hesitate. "It's just, breastfeeding requires, you know. Breasts. I didn't want to just whip them out and you panic."

"Leila Grace, I need you to look at me and listen very carefully."

I do.

"You are providing nourishment to our daughter with your body. Not every woman can, and not every woman wants to. But you've chosen to. If anyone gives you shit for it, you knee them in the balls then let me know so that I can lay them out, too. Got me?"

"Yes, sir," I say before I can stop myself.

He huffs a breath and looks away, but I still catch the way his cheeks redden, the way his pupils dilate. Clearing his throat, he shifts to the conversation we need to have while I settle in the recliner.

Kaia eagerly latches on as soon as I offer her a nipple, and when I look up, I'm surprised to find Drew studying my face. I figured his eyes would be on the exposed breast, but of course he's too good of a guy to look where he shouldn't.

"I know I've said it, but I'm sorry for not being there for any of this."

"I know you are."

"I didn't listen to your voicemails until the other morning. Or read your texts. I told myself it was for the best." He pauses for a second, as if to gather his thoughts. "I was…not in the best mental state right after everything happened."

"I know, it's—"

"Let me finish. Please," he says, cutting me off. "I'd already worked it out with my dad to come back up. He gave me a long weekend. You sent me a text, worrying about how to tell Gavin that we'd been sneaking around under his nose for years. Then I started worrying, scared you'd decide it wasn't worth the trouble. That I wasn't worth the trouble."

"Drew, no," I whisper.

"Then I made stupid choices that should've cost me my life and almost cost a perfectly good horse his. Then I ignored you. Left you on your own when you needed me."

"Gavin wanted to tell Declan, but I didn't want to pressure you into this. You didn't ask for this responsibility," I say, nodding down at Kaia. "I considered all the options in depth and knew I couldn't live with myself if I wasn't the one raising her. Even if I had to do it alone." I look up at Drew and offer a watery smile. "Would it have been easier if you'd been at appointments with me or in the delivery room or helping during the nights since she's been born? Sure. But I honestly wasn't sure if you'd checked your messages or if you—" I cut myself off, because, in my gut, I know the thoughts I had about why he never called or showed up weren't accurate. Still, Drew keys into my thoughts, his entire body sagging in defeat.

"I will never stop apologizing for missing so much time. But, Leila, hear me when I say this. I would have been there if I had known. And now that I do? She'll never know a day without me again."

I nod, unable to form the words I want to say. I shouldn't need to hear those words out loud, but relief soars through me anyway.

"Did Gavin at least go with you?" he asks. "I hate to think you had to do anything by yourself."

"Yeah, he's been there for everything. The dude's a freakin' saint, Drew. He has to be tired of me." Sighing, I lean my head back and stare at the ceiling fan as it slowly spins. I rub at my eyes, hoping like hell the moisture gathering doesn't leak over. I'm exhausted.

"What can I do, right now, to lighten the load for you?"

I choke on a wet laugh, silently apologizing to Kaia as I displace her suction. Helping her relatch, I look back at Drew, expecting to see...I don't know what.

Shaking my head, I shrug one shoulder before letting it drop heavily. Words don't come as emotions threaten to spill over. Without a word, Drew is up and dropping to his knees before me. His fingers wrap around my calves, squeezing lightly as he looks up at me through thick lashes. I suck a breath as his deep blues stare through my defenses.

"What are you doing?" I whisper, the words so quiet he probably wouldn't hear them if he wasn't this close.

His eyes flick to our daughter as she pops off of me. "Will she nap for a while?"

"In theory, if I can transfer her without waking her."

"Does she have somewhere other than your room?"

"The nursery is set up. We just don't really use it much yet. Why?"

"Go lay her down in there then come back out here," he says softly, giving another squeeze to my legs before standing and offering me a hand.

"Drew."

"Don't argue, sunshine." The set of his jaw and the determination in his gaze stop me from saying anything more as I stand and do as he says. Kaia wiggles a little but settles once I tuck a light blanket around her hips. I'm sure she'll kick it off in no time, but it always makes her feel secure during her naps since she isn't swaddled.

"She settled?" Drew asks as I walk back to him.

I lift the hand with the monitor in it to show him that she's peacefully sleeping.

He nods, pulling me into his arms and dropping a kiss on my forehead. "Now, you're going to go take a hot shower or a bath and not worry about her," he says, slipping the monitor from my fingers.

Chapter 10
Drew

I can almost see the wheels turning in Leila's head as she considers my command. The second she opens her mouth to argue against it, I cover her lips with my thumb.

"Shower or bath. I don't care which. Stand under hot water, soak in it, daydream, shave, read a book. Whatever you want." I spin her to face the hallway and swat her butt. "Go. Now."

She huffs as she walks away, and I swear I hear her whisper "bossy cowboy" as she closes her bedroom door.

I grin at her retreating form. She hasn't changed a lick. Honestly, she's probably even more stubborn now that she has someone else to look out for. Leila Grace has always been a force to be reckoned with. She's fiery, strong, and one of the goodest people I know. Everything she went through as a teen would have ruined most. I know she still has nightmares, but she came out on top. She'd still give the shirt off her back, step in whenever it's needed.

But the girl needs to take care of herself.

I know she thinks she only closed her eyes for a second when she was nursing, but those gorgeous greens stayed closed for several minutes as she dozed off. It wasn't until Kaia kicked a little foot that she snapped awake and I moved forward to kneel before her.

I wait until I hear water running in the pipes to start doing what I can to help straighten up. It isn't *messy*, but I don't want Leila dealing with dirty dishes or swapping the laundry. It only takes a minute to fold the clean towel load and switch the wash to the dryer, but I hesitate on starting a new load until I find the laundry detergent with a baby on the front. Dumping the basket of tiny garments in and adding the soap, I cross my fingers nothing in there is supposed to skip the wash.

The little monitor stays glued to my hand as I move through the house, tidying anything I can. Just as I'm about to sneak into the nursery to watch Kaia sleep, the front door opens, my brother's best friend coming home.

"Figured that was your truck out front," Gavin says as he kicks off his sneakers and slips into his boots. "Where're the girls?"

I lift the monitor to show him a sleeping Kaia. "Leila is in the shower, sounds like. She's supposed to be relaxing."

He nods. "How'd you manage that?"

"Didn't give her a choice."

He chuckles. "Bet she loved that."

"She dozed off while breastfeeding. Declan said you wanted to talk to me?"

"Yeah. Moreso just checking in. I know this was unexpected."

I shrug. "We'll piece it all together as we go."

"How's your recovery going?" he asks, gesturing to my left side.

"Eh. Is what it is. Not healing like the doc wants it to and needs another round of surgery, but I said no."

He nods again, his chin tucked, but his eyes cut up to me. "And the other thing?"

Not gonna lie. It'll never quit hurting when the people in my life show any disappointment in me.

"Clean. Swear it. I wouldn't come around otherwise."

"Good, good." He steps toward the key rack on the wall and pulls off a singular key before tossing it to me. "I'm in and out. Going to meet your brother and shoot the shit, maybe hit the trails. Kaia wakes up at four every morning like clockwork. In case you're interested." He turns the knob to open the door again.

"That's it?" I ask. I more than deserve at least a punch to the face from this guy, but instead he just nods.

"For now." And with that, Gavin slips back out the door, closing it gently.

I stare at the door, convinced I imagined that encounter. But when I squeeze my fist, the house key cuts into my palm.

***

The big man upstairs must have a warped sense of humor. Not ten minutes after the strange encounter with Gavin, a door in the hallway creaks and a soft voice whispers, "Hey, Drew?"

Poking my head around, I see Leila's head peeking around the edge of the door. "You okay?"

"Um, I may have forgotten to grab a towel."

Of course, she did because I just folded five of them. Stepping into the laundry room, I pick the fluffiest one and take it to her, making sure to keep my eyes averted as she opens the door enough to slip the towel through before shutting it quickly.

It doesn't matter if I don't actually catch a glimpse, though.

Leila's figure is engrained in my mind. From her strong, athletic calves to her thick thighs. The ass and hips that, even filled out from bringing life to our child, are still perfection and would fill my hands even better than before. That cute little waist of hers up to her now-full breasts. The scars she pretends don't exist. I memorized every inch of her body in the years we snuck around.

I accepted a long time ago that the memories are all I'll ever have.

Before the past can drag me down, a whimper travels through the monitor. The nursery is at the far end of the hall, and while I know they've only had a short while to get it put together, the room is perfect for our princess. Three soft-pink walls meet with a single navy wall, KAIA in cream-colored lettering centered over the white crib. A matching dresser and rocker are against the opposite wall, a flowy pink-and-white curtain completing the room.

Kaia's little body wiggles as she tries to eat her fist, little suckling noises bringing a smile to my lips. Gently, and with only a touch of hesitation on if I'm qualified for this, I lift her, ignoring the twinges in my shoulder. I'm going to snuggle my daughter post-nap, damn it. Keeping her head cradled, I shift her until she's snuggled under my chin and happily smacking on her fingers.

"You're the perfect baby, aren't you, precious?" I murmur, loving the way she feels in my arms. I gently sway, hoping to keep her from fussing for at least a little longer. "Never knew I could fall in love at first sight twice. But what do you know? You and your mama have that in common. Two perfect girls stuck with a not-so-perfect me. But I'll do my best for you. For both of you. I swear it."

Chapter 11
Leila

I should be ashamed of myself for eavesdropping on Drew and Kaia, but I couldn't help it. He'd set the monitor on the table at the end of the hall. It's almost too much. The way he holds her so naturally, the slight sway of his body as he whispers promises to her. The reminder of what we could have. Our own little family of three like we'd always planned.

Could we get back to that? I'm strong enough to admit that my feelings for Drew never disappeared. It's the trust, the fear of losing him again, that keeps me from telling him as much when I silently slip into the nursery and step into his line of sight, monitor in my hand.

It doesn't take but a second for him to piece it together.

"It's true, you know," Drew whispers, keeping his eyes on the little girl who looks so much like her daddy already. Same unruly hair, blue eyes that I hope don't change color, and a little dimple in her right cheek. "How was your shower?" he asks, finally glancing up.

"Much needed," I admit. "Thank you."

His head shakes before I finish talking. "Helping you take care of yourself isn't something to thank me for. It should be a given."

Not wanting to argue, I shrug before silencing the monitor and setting it on Kaia's dresser.

"Still up for going to meet up with everyone? I know you're exhausted, so if you'd rather just crash—"

"We're going out, Drew. I know you want to show this cutie off," I say as I tickle the bottom of Kaia's foot.

When he asks if I'm sure, I cut my eyes at him, eyebrow raised. "Just let me change her diaper and we can go."

"Alright, sunshine."

***

The lights are low as we enter Jace Riley's Bar and Grill, a soft country tune playing through the speakers. A handful of patrons are scattered throughout, but it's mostly vacant. I guess that's what happens at three o'clock on a weekday.

"Are you sure her face is okay like this, Leila?" Drew asks, fidgeting with the baby wrap he insisted on using as he leads me to the bar stools at the back of the room.

Chuckling even as nerves consume my entire being, I rest a hand on his waist. "Promise. She likes to bury her face, but her nose and mouth aren't smooshed against you." Glancing up through my lashes, I watch him watch Kaia. "She just feels secure and loved," I whisper, my lips ticking.

His eyes shoot to me, some unreadable expression dashing across his face before a sweet smile settles on his lips.

"Right. Let's get you reacquainted with everyone." He slips a hand behind me, resting it on my lower back before guiding me to the small group of people gathered at the far end of the bar. Kelsey and Jett are splitting an order of fries while the two guys seem to be studying something on the shorter one's phone.

"Since I know the gigantic dude is Jace, I'm guessing the other one is Noah."

"Yep."

"Was he around back then?" Back when my life was crumbling. Back when I didn't notice much of anything because I was more focused on flying under the radar.

Drew nods. "You probably didn't cross paths too often. He was usually with Jace but didn't really talk to anyone back then. He was dealing with his own hell."

"Loner. Gotcha. And he's Jett's?"

Drew laughs out loud, drawing the attention of the four. "Yeah, Noah belongs to Jett." He says it loud enough that the others hear, and Jett beams with satisfaction at the claiming. Noah's face tinges with pink, but to his credit, he doesn't back down.

"She sleeping?" Jace asks, wiping his hands on a white rag while nodding toward Kaia.

"Out like a light," Drew boasts.

"Don't get too excited," Kelsey says. "She's likely to wake up as the afternoon crowd livens up the place."

"Kels is right," I say.

"She's in that thing?" Noah asks, finally glancing up. "I thought it was another shoulder brace." His face goes from curious to concerned faster than I can track. "You didn't walk here did you? Sun'll be going down before—"

Jett cuts him off with a hand on his cheek. "What've we talked about, elevator man?"

He sighs heavily, eyes rolling but looking perfectly chastised. "That there's nothing wrong with the sidewalks around town."

"And?"

"And I shouldn't tell grown-ass men where they can and can't walk."

"And?"

Noah's face softens as Jett's expression takes on a teasing edge. "And you're the most beautiful girl in the room, chaos," he says, leaning into Jett. Their noses brush in a sweet almost kiss.

Some random patron yells for them to get a room, but everyone laughs good naturedly.

I can tell this conversation is way over my head, but Drew eases Noah's concerns. "We drove, man. I just strapped her to me outside because there's not really room for a stroller in here. Besides, do you see how freaking sexy I look in this thing?" He puts a hand on his hip and kicks his butt out, imaginary hair flip included. "I'm gorgeous."

Noah and Jace snort laughter while the girls roll their eyes.

Jace looks at me. "Been a long time, Leila. How's it been being a mom?"

"Like nothing I imagined," I say honestly. "Still learning. Always tired, but I wouldn't trade it for the world."

He nods. "I get that. Want something to eat? Buck makes a mean plate of cowboy nachos."

"What's that?" I ask, scrunching my nose.

"Only the best thing you'll ever put in your mouth," pipes Jett.

Noah scoffs at his girlfriend's response. "I take offense to that, ma'am."

"None of that shit at my bar," Jace groans. "This is a public eatery, and not all of Havenwood wants to know about your birthday suit shenanigans."

I notice a few patrons glance our way, and Jace's ears turn pink as he realizes more people heard him than Jett's comment.

"You're just jealous you aren't gettin' any, little brother," Kelsey chimes in, never one to leave well enough alone.

"By three minutes, and neither are you."

A knowing glint fills Kelsey's eyes as she takes a bite of another fry before pointing the remaining portion at her twin. "Hmm, keep thinkin' that, bubs."

I hide my giggle behind my hand while Drew coughs to cover his laughter.

Jace throws his hands up, clearly exasperated with his sister. "Know what? Forget it. I'm going to the kitchen. I'll come back when you guys grow up."

"He's just salty because he's lonely. All he does is work and go home to that huge empty house," Kelsey says.

"Wait, wasn't he engaged right at the end of your senior year? Whatever happened to her?" I ask.

The collective silence from the group makes me regret opening my mouth. Clearly, nothing good came of it.

"We've all seen our share of hurt over the years, sunshine," Drew says before placing a chaste kiss on the top of my head.

Jett reaches for my arm, pulling me closer to her and Kelsey. I can't help but glance back over at Drew, but he's already in discussion with Noah, steadily bouncing on his feet. His large, calloused hand rests against the back of Kaia's head protectively.

"Somebody's swooning," says Kelsey, a grin plastered to her face.

I jump, suddenly aware of my staring. "What? No."

"Mhmm. Whatever you say, Lala."

"Lala?" Jett asks.

I roll my eyes, sliding into the open stool next to them. "My brother's childhood nickname for me. Kels thinks she can use it because she's got an in with the guardian."

Kelsey snorts. "Just because my best friend is back in town after a decade doesn't mean anything. You've been 'Lala' since the day you were born."

"I forget you guys all grew up here sometimes. Me and Noah are the odd balls," Jett says.

Kelsey shifts gears. "So, how are things really going? You guys settling in okay? Gav said you were still set on moving somewhere on your own."

I nod. "I haven't started looking yet."

"You know, Noah's got a few rentals. You could ask him if any are available," Jett mentions.

"I might. I just want to get out of Gavin's hair, you know?"

"Your brother wants you there, Leila," Kelsey reassures me.

I shrug. "He's been taking care of me for over a decade now. It's time I figure out how to go out on my own. As soon as I figure out what to do about a job."

"I thought you were working that remote gig?" Kelsey asks.

"I was. But they wanted me to start coming into the office twice a week once my leave was up. Not really possible now that I'm in a different state."

"You were doing admin stuff, right?"

"More or less. Scheduling, prepping documents."

She looks at Jett. "Still wanting to hire an assistant?"

Jett's eyes light up as she swings to me. "You're hired!"

"Wait, what?" I look between Jett and Kelsey as I feel Drew's heat at my back. "You don't even know me."

"I don't need to. Kelsey knows you, and she's the one who gave me my shot a few months ago."

Drew's hand settles on my waist as he says, "Jett's a special kind of crazy, but she's our crazy."

"He's right. When I moved here at the beginning of the year, I was running from myself. My head is a chaotic mess ninety-eight percent of the time, but this town helped me chase what I thought was a far-fetched idea. Now, I'm running a bookstore café alongside my editing services. It's taken off, and I need someone who can keep me organized and on track with deadlines."

When I don't answer immediately, she smiles. "Think about it. You can work remote most of the time, and if you need to come in, baby girl is always welcome."

"I don't want a pity job."

"It's not. I swear it. I've been meaning to post the position on some of those job sites, but I keep forgetting until two in the morning."

"If you're sure."

"Absolutely. And no rush on starting. Feel free to take a few more weeks."

I shake my head. "If you're sure, I'd love to start next week."

"Cool beans. We can talk more about it later."

Jace steps back around the corner and slides a plate of tater tots with what looks like shredded chicken and barbeque sauce on top. "What's your beverage of choice?"

"Sweet tea would be heavenly."

"You good?" Drew asks softly.

I nod. "It's kind of nice being around people again."

His eyebrows furrow. "I thought you had support in Tennessee?"

Shaking my head, I shrug. "I had Gavin. Kristen when I needed her. That was enough."

"From now on, you have this town, this group right here. And you have me. No more doing this on your own," he whispers against my hair before dropping a kiss to the top of

And don't try to tell me that my thoughts are irrational. I know the statistics of SIDS, and it is one of my biggest fears as a mother.

It's why I breathe a sigh of relief when I see her bassinet empty. The logical parts of my brain finally kick on, and I realize Gavin probably came in to get her when he woke up. It's not unusual for him to steal her for snuggles in the mornings. I just usually hear him come in.

What I definitely don't expect is to walk into the kitchen and find Drew Flynn at the counter preparing a bottle with one hand while the other holds Kaia against his chest.

Why does it feel like my insides are melting every time I see this man doing the simplest of things? Watching him warm a bottle of breastmilk should not be a turn on.

He startles when he sees me. "Oh, shit. Crap. Snap! Sorry, I don't know what the protocol is for cursing around babies."

"She's heard it all. Besides, it's kind of cute watching you freak out over your swear word vocabulary."

"I didn't hear you come in. You sleep okay?"

"Mhmm." I walk closer, cocking my hip out as I lean against the refrigerator. "What are you doing here, Drew?"

"Just spending time with my daughter before the day gets busy."

"And the blanket and pillow on the couch?"

"We had a snuggle sesh?"

One brow raises as I wait for him to continue.

He finally sighs. "Gavin gave me a key and insinuated that you weren't getting much sleep."

"He did, did he?"

It's his turn to stare me down. "So, after I dropped you guys off last night, I went home to change and grab clothes for today before texting Gavin that I'd sneak in once y'all had gone to bed. He left a blanket out for me. Probably really for Kaia, but I used it."

My chest squeezes at the casualness of his tone, like he doesn't think it's a big deal that he just gave me my first night of sleep in almost a year. Like he didn't just fully immerse himself in the parent role that I prayed he'd want to fill. The constant guilt I feel at not coming back sooner tries to seep in. If I'd been brave enough to show up months ago, he would have been there for us. I one thousand percent know that now.

"So, did it work?" he asks while I'm lost in my head, in the *could haves* and *what ifs*.

"Hmm?"

"Did you get more sleep than normal?"

"I did. Until I woke up in a panic because I'd slept so good."

He winces. "Sorry. Again."

"Don't be. I'm...I needed it." Lord knows the bags under my eyes were dark enough to count as a black eye these days. I bet I could sleep for another six hours or so if given the option, but I don't tell Drew that. He has Kaia tilted like a pro, making sure she doesn't get any air bubbles in the nipple.

It's crazy to think this is the same guy who just a few days ago was terrified of holding her when I threw her into his arms. The same guy who is making it more and more difficult to protect my heart from.

I knew coming to Havenwood would be risky. I'm starting to think I didn't consider all the possible scenarios. Like my heart still belonging solely to the man in front of me.

Because I am one hundred percent still in love with Drew Flynn. And I don't know if I want to fight it anymore.

"We should probably continue our conversation from yesterday," he says after a minute of us both watching Kaia. Even as he speaks to me, he only has eyes for her.

I step forward to take the now empty bottle from him and move to the sink, washing it to give my hands something to do. "What else is there to say? We both made choices, and we're living with the consequences. We'll figure out the rest as we go."

"You didn't ask anything about why I left. Or about the pills. I know you know about them."

Sighing, I set the clean bottle and nipple on the counter and turn around. My back rests against the coolness of the oversize farm sink as I think of a response.

"Are you actively popping pain pills?"

"No."

"Are you planning to do anything to jeopardize the safety of our daughter?"

"Of course not. She's everything."

"Then I don't have any questions. I trust you, Drew."

"Even if I told you I almost messed up the day you came to town?"

"See, I'm not concerned about the almost." Sliding my hand along the arm not cradling Kaia, I step closer. "I almost died when my stepdad shot me. But I didn't give up. I almost lost hope in humanity, but certain people in my life reminded me that, where there's darkness, there's also light. I almost stayed in Tennessee, but we wouldn't have been able to raise Kaia together."

His body shudders on an exhale, and I know if I looked up that his eyes would be closed as he chokes back the emotion roiling through him. Instead, I keep my eyes on our daughter as she sleeps contentedly in her father's arms. Something I'll never regret allowing.

"You *almost* messed up, but you didn't. I'm betting you either sought out Jace or your brother because you knew they'd have your back. The *almost* doesn't matter, because you're here, and you'll do everything you can to stay here and healthy for the little girl in your arms."

Chapter 13
Drew

She doesn't know it, but Leila Barrett just ruined me with those words. This girl has always been and will always be the only woman capable of bringing me to my knees.

Well, I guess Kaia will, too, as she gets older and learns the power she has over her old man.

Just one look from either of them has me wanting to make every wish come true.

It's in this moment that I realize one hard truth: I'll do whatever it takes to earn Leila's heart.

"I don't know what to say to any of that. Except things you probably aren't ready to hear." It's so tempting to spill those three little words and beg her to let me love her, but I know better.

"You don't need to say anything."

"You still good to come to family dinner tonight? Mom's been blowing up my phone all morning about it. She's already made an extra-large banana pudding."

"As long as you're sure they aren't disappointed in me. I'm sure your dad isn't thrilled about the situation, either."

"They know it's not on you. They love you, and Dad is more than ready to meet his granddaughter."

Leila reaches for Kaia, gently settling her into the crook of her elbow. "I need morning snuggles. Feels wrong without it," she says, looking only slightly sorry.

"No worries. I have an appointment to get to, anyway," I say as I notice the time on the stove.

She glances up at me worriedly.

"Just a checkup."

Skepticism stays on her face, and I can't fault her for it.

"Would you tell me if it was more?" she asks.

Sighing, I run a hand through my hair. "Some of my shoulder injuries didn't heal. I'm trying to avoid more surgeries. It's constant inflammation since I went back to riding and working out, even though the use is minimal."

"I expect you to tell me what the doctor says," she says, one eyebrow raised as if daring me to argue.

"Yes, ma'am. Full report coming your way."

"Don't be a smartass. I need to know if you're not supposed to hold ten pounds on that side so I can kick your butt if you aren't taking care of yourself."

"Promise I'll let you know what she says." I glance at the clock. "But I do need to go before I'm late."

She shoos me, but I still lean forward and place a kiss on Kaia's head before doing the same to Leila. "I'll pick you guys up at four for dinner."

"See you then."

As soon as my boots hit the porch, I have my phone to my ear. It rings twice before Noah answers.

"Yeah," he says, rarely one for words.

I cut straight to the chase. "That little farmhouse I bought from you—"

He cuts me off. "Already dropped the keys and alarm code off at your loft."

I freeze halfway into my truck. I haven't mentioned it to him in months. Hell, I never picked up the keys because of everything that happened. "How'd you know?"

"Had a feeling. Just had cleaners go through last week, so it's ready for move in. Pretty sure Jett stocked the fridge and cabinets yesterday, too."

"Thanks, man."

"Sure thing, bud," he says before ending the call.

Shaking my head at my buddy's intuition, I climb the rest of the way into my truck and start the engine.

One task down. A million more to go.

***

"Let me be one thousand percent crystal clear, Drew," says Dr. Lindsey, her voice stern, just like every other time she's given me this same spiel. "You need to get this inflammation under control. The longer you let it build, the less likely it is it'll ever improve."

I look away from her no-nonsense stare, instead studying the bland color scheme of the exam room. Different shades of tan coat the walls, floor, and cabinets in soul-sucking boredom. My newest set of X-rays are visible on the monitor next to Dr. Lindsey's petite frame. She's been the only ortho in Havenwood for over a decade, and she's damn good at her job. That doesn't mean I don't want to bolt at the first mention of having to see her.

She taps away on her keyboard, ignoring my bouts of panic as she tries to fill a new prescription for me. "I'm sending over 800 milligram ibuprofen tablets. Three a day for a week, one every eight hours."

My head is shaking before she gets the third word out. Refusing to make eye contact, I say, "No. I can't risk it."

She looks up from her laptop, a sympathetic look already gracing her features. "Ibuprofen is safe for you to take, Drew. I wouldn't prescribe it if I thought it would cause issues for you, but your body needs healing. It can't heal if it keeps attacking itself."

A groan slips out as I rub rough fingers along the back of my neck. Between the last few weeks—hell, months—and the increasing ache in my shoulder, a knot of tension has created a new home at the base my skull. "What other options do I have?" I ask even though I already know the answer.

Dr. Lindsey's expression says it all. "You've exhausted every non-surgical option, Drew. You'll be back in my operating room within the next six months if this"—she motions to my left side—"doesn't get the rest it needs."

"So, realistically, what are my options?" I can't keep my frustration from seeping into my voice. I'd finally been cleared by my physical therapist to go back to my daily activities. Those activities include boxing and training horses. Can I live without the boxing? Probably. I'd miss it, but I can find other avenues for stress release.

She sighs. "Ice often, immobilize it whenever you're out and about. I will offer you one, and only one, cortisol shot, but you'll have to agree to take it easy for a few days." She holds a hand up before I have a chance to interrupt her. "Non-negotiable. If I do this, you ice like crazy and wear your brace for the next three days. No boxing, no training rides. If you can't do it comfortably in a brace, you are to avoid it. Got me?"

"Yes, ma'am," I grumble as I try my best to remember where I threw my sling-like shoulder brace the other day. Dr. Lindsey walks out the door, letting me know a tech will prep the shot. I breathe in, trying to cleanse my body of any extra tension as the door closes while fighting the stress that builds with every passing moment.

I slip my phone from my pocket and open my messages, studying the names that sit at the top of my text app. With an unsteady hand, I tap the third name then type out a text and hit send before I can talk myself out of it.

Drew: Doc says no gym or rides 3 days.

Almost immediately, my phone buzzes with a reply, my brother's name filling the notification bubble.

Declan: I'll be out front.

Several minutes pass before a tech with graying hair and laugh lines walks in with a needle and syringe, and my insides draw up tight at the sight of it. That's one big-ass needle.

"Hey, sweetie, my name's Tris." She starts simple chatter as she gathers a prep pad and Band-Aid before making her way to my injured shoulder. "We've mixed the cortisone with a numbing agent, so you should feel at least a little relief pretty quick." She lifts the back hem of my shirt over my shoulder. "Hold this in place, hun."

I move my right hand to hold the shirt out of her way as she swipes the alcohol wipe over my shoulder.

"You're going to feel a pinch and maybe some burning. Deep breath."

I've barely sucked in any oxygen when the needle hits home. My jaw clenches as any air that had been in my lungs rushes right back out. "Warning would'a been nice," I grumble as I try my best to keep still. Whatever is in the syringe burns as it settles.

"If I'd warned ya, you would've tensed."

"Valid point."

A quick knock on the door sounds before Dr. Lindsey sticks her head back inside as Tris disposes of her supplies. "Do I need to call your father and tell him your orders, or can I trust you to follow directions this time?"

"I followed directions last time. I did the physical therapy. PT cleared me to go back to work." A lot of good it did me.

Dr. Lindsey cuts her eyes at me, and I sigh, utterly defeated by a nearly year-old injury.

"Be boring for three days. Got it," I deadpan.

Dr. Lindsey can't quite keep the grin from tugging up her lips. "Quit being smart, boy. I'll call your entire support system if I need to."

"Really, I've got it," I promise as I stand from the exam table. "I already texted Declan, anyway."

"You've got an entire town that cares about you. And, from what I've heard through the gossipy grapevine, it's grown by three recently," she says as I walk out the door. "Don't forget that."

"Yes, ma'am."

I walk out the front door of the physician's building to greet Declan on the sidewalk. I know what his text said, but I'm still surprised to find him right outside the doors waiting on a bench.

"What do you need from me, little brother?" he asks. There is no irritation from our earlier conversation, no *I told you so* on the shoulder problem. Just *what do you need?* like how it used to be between us.

My lip curls upward at the thought, but I can't hold on to it. "I need an outlet since both of mine were just ripped away for three days, and I need something to keep me busy so I don't annoy Leila all afternoon. You decide."

We head across the street to the middle of the square. We're actually standing under Declan and Kristen's tree where their engagement photos were taken. The magnolia tree is over one hundred years old and a favorite for picnics and pictures of milestones like graduation.

"So, aside from what you texted me, what other rules did she give you?" asks my brother.

"Lots of ice and wear my brace."

"Should we go back to your place and get it?"

I laugh, not because it's funny but because this entire situation is a mess. "Dude, I don't even know where it is at this point."

Declan rolls his eyes. "Of course not." He looks around at the shops and businesses along Main Street before moving toward the ice cream shop that is next to Riley's.

"Ice cream? Really?"

Declan holds his hands out, palms up and with childlike innocence. "When is ice cream ever a bad idea? Besides, you clearly didn't have any better ones."

I nod. "Fair point."

Declan steps up to the window to order, and I take in the sights of our little town. I've lived here all my life, but I never get tired of the people or the peace the quiet brings. When Declan hands me a cone of double fudge ice cream, I sigh.

"I'm sorry about earlier. You're just trying to look out for me, and I'm grasping at straws with Leila. I know you think it's stupid, but I still love her."

He takes a bite of his strawberry cheesecake ice cream before pointing his spoon at me. "It's not stupid, bro. I just don't want to see you get hurt again."

We start the trek back to my apartment in order to search for the elusive brace.

"I'm going to ask her to move in with me."

Declan looks shocked, but to his credit, he doesn't say anything.

"That little farm house on the backside of Mom and Dad's yard? I bought it from Dad over a year ago. Picked out a ring and asked Gavin for his blessing."

Drew sighs heavily, and I silently plead with whoever is listening that my brother is willing to help me make this happen. He continues eating his ice cream, a contemplative look on his face as if he's trying to work out where this is going.

"So, Gavin knew you were together. You were ready to propose. And I pushed you away from her? What the hell, man?"

"I'd hit you if I had two usable arms and this ice cream wasn't the best damn thing I've tasted all day." Of course, he'll still try to blame himself for my decisions. "Look, I already told you earlier, I made the choice to not go back. To not check my messages. I should've put Leila first back then. I'm going to from now on, until the day I die. But I need your help."

This time when he sighs, I know I've got him. "What do you need from me, kid?"

I fill him in on the plan I've been working on since last night as we make our way into my apartment above the gym. It'll take all our friends to pull this off...and that's *if* I can convince Leila to go for it.

Glancing at the clock above the stove, I groan. It's already two. "All I want to do is sleep, but I promised Mom we'd be at family dinner tonight."

Declan sets about filling a plastic bag with ice before handing it to me since my array of ice packs are all sitting on the counter instead of in the freezer. "Sit down and ice. Where should I look for the brace first?"

I sink into the cool leather of my recliner and settle the ice pack over the top of my shoulder. "Check the basket in the closet that has my belts in it."

I hear the closet door open and close before he mutters, "Not there."

"What about under the bathroom cabinet?"

He steps across the hall, and rummages through the small storage area. "Winner, winner."

The ice isn't cold enough to reach the inferno under my shirt, so I slip the bag through the collar of my shirt, wincing at the contact. The lidocaine that had been mixed with the shot numbed some of the area for a bit, but it's no match for the heat already seeping through. It'd be pretty neat if the gigantic needle I just suffered through could result in even a few days of relief.

When Declan walks back in and hands me the brace, I slip it over my head before tucking my elbow into the sling portion and tightening the strap that sits across my chest. Declan resituates the ice pack once I'm settled back into my chair.

"If you need the rest, Mom would understand postponing for a day or two," he says.

"You're probably right, but you didn't see her when she met Kaia. It's like it finally clicked that their favorite child is back in town." Leila has always held a special place in my parents' hearts, and it devastated them when she left and never called. Having her back—with their first grandchild in tow—is too important to them for me to try postponing.

"I'm sure meeting her first grandchild made her pretty ecstatic." The flash of regret is there and gone, covered by Declan's usual expression, and I fight the urge to apologize because he and Kristen have always wanted a little one of their own.

I do my best to change the subject. "I don't want to be stuck in this apartment all by myself. I'm not allowed downstairs, and with this amount of pent-up energy, it's a recipe for disaster. And if we skip dinner, it means telling Mom and Dad *why* I need to reschedule it." Dad has been hesitant enough with me riding again as it is.

Declan changes the subject by asking, "You ever reach back out to Gavin? He joining us tonight?"

"No, I didn't. I guess I should before I head over there. But I think he's going to Kelsey's."

Declan chuckles knowingly. "Alright. I need to get back to the barn to at least put those others on the hotwalker. You sure you're good?"

I nod. "Promise."

"You're welcome to come hang out at the barn or head over to the house if you'd rather. Kristen and the pup are there."

"I know, Dec." But I won't be taking him up on his offer. I've already missed so much time with Kaia, even if she won't remember these days. If I have the opportunity to spend time with her, I'll choose her. Always.

Declan lets himself out as I locate my phone to call Gavin. He picks up on the third ring.

When his grumbly voice comes on the line, I start talking. "Hey, sorry about not getting back to you sooner. It's been a crazy day."

"No worries. Just wanted to tell you that Leila probably won't be up for much."

My stomach churns as I immediately consider all the things that could've gone wrong today. "She okay? Is she hurt? Kaia?" I ramble on, but Gavin cuts me off before I can ask more.

"She had a small panic attack earlier, and it set her on edge. The adrenaline crash hit hard, so she's napping."

"Kaia?" I ask, already grabbing my keys and making my way out the door.

"Playing with her toes right now."

"On my way."

Chapter 14
Leila

"Knock, knock."

The soft padding of feet approaches my bed. I continue to face the wall, my navy weighted blanket pulled to my chin. It feels like there's a cinder block pressing against my chest and a post-panic-attack headache pulses against my temples.

My bed dips before Drew's fingers gently massage my scalp. "Hey, sunshine. How ya feeling?"

I keep quiet, knowing he doesn't want the answer I'd give. He's witnessed enough of my post-panic episodes to know how closed-off I get.

In Drew fashion, he doesn't let my silence faze him, just keeps talking like I'm not ignoring his presence. "Your brother said he'd take Kaia for a stroll while we get you into a warm shower and decompress."

I sink deeper into the mattress, not wanting to face him. What he must think of me as a mother, passing our kid off to her uncle because I can't handle my own mental health.

Drew's hand tightens in my hair as he pulls lightly. It isn't painful, just enough to regain my focus.

"Come on, sunshine. Up you go," he says as he peels my blanket from my grip. He gingerly rolls me to face him, and the worry in his blue eyes hits deep. He shouldn't need to worry about me like this.

His hands grasp mine and tug until I'm on my feet. With an arm around my waist, he leads me to the bathroom where steam already billows from the shower, a lavender shower scent spreading the relaxing aroma though the room. Drew lets go of me long enough to test the water, and I immediately lean against the sink.

When he turns back to me, I do my best to force a smile. "It's a great idea, but I'm not steady enough to stand in the shower right now. Maybe later." I turn to start making my way to bed when Drew's corded muscles wrap around my waist.

"Standing under running water always helps you recharge. This one clearly hit harder than you let on to your brother, and

I *should* take you over my knee for lying to him about it. As it is"—he turns me to face him before brushing back the section of hair that slipped free during my burrowing session—"you need this. So, you can either get in on your own, or I can step in with you."

My cheeks heat at the image of past showers. Of his hands gliding over every inch of my skin. The press of his body to mine.

Drew's hand squeezes my neck, the pressure grounding me, keeping me from slipping too deep into the past. I try to brush off the emotions that surge with the memories, but the joke falls flat. "Are you sure you don't just want to see me naked?"

Instead of shying away, Drew raises an eyebrow as his lips quirk up in a smirk. "I'm always up for admiring your beauty, sunshine, but you're deflecting."

I snort. "Hilarious. You can't honestly tell me you want to see this two-month postpartum body in all it's stretched, fatty, unsexy glory."

"We really gonna do this right now?"

"Do what right now?"

He sighs. "You know what."

"I don't have the energy for this right now," I say as I try to step out of his arms.

"Too bad." He turns me to face the mirror, one arm still holding me steady while the other glides over my oversize Steele

Valley Voltage hockey shirt, both of us ignoring the fact that it belonged to Drew at some point. When he grazes my stomach, I can't help but flinch at the mental flood.

"I'm not the same girl from that night in your hotel room," I whisper, the words barely audible.

He slides both arms around me. One rests between my aching breasts, his hand settling on my throat. Not squeezing, but comforting, just how I need. It isn't fair that this man knows all the right buttons. The other arm settles around my waist, calloused hand splayed across my stomach in such a possessive move that my head goes fuzzy.

Drew presses a kiss to the top of my head. "Damn straight, you aren't." He lifts the edge of my shirt, and my breath catches but I don't stop him. "Arms up," he whispers.

He slips the shirt over my head as I follow his gentle demand, baring all of me since I'd stripped my panties and bra before crawling into bed. His hands never stop stroking my skin—stomach, arms, shoulders—as he continues in that soft, rumbly voice that belongs in a sexy audiobook. "Maybe it won't happen today, tomorrow, or next week. But at some point, you'll look in the mirror and see how badass you are. How amazing this body is for creating and carrying life."

I suck a breath at the sincerity reflected back to me in the steamed mirror. I bite my lower lip as I gather the courage to turn and face the man of my dreams.

I thought these feelings only existed in fairytales.

Instead of admitting to the thoughts in my head, I peek up through my lashes to find Drew watching me closely. "I made a promise to myself before coming back. That I was done hiding and wanted to live my life brighter and braver than I have over the last decade. My innocence may have been stripped away, but they aren't here anymore. I am."

Drew drops a kiss to my forehead and whispers, "I'm proud of you, Leila Grace."

That does it. Right there. I knew coming back would open me up to old wounds, but I didn't consider how my heart might crack open again. Or maybe I did. I don't know. But the fact that the man I love, the only man I've ever loved, is proud of me? The tears start, and I don't even try to hide them. I know who I am. I know what I've survived. But having my struggles be validated by someone as special as Drew Flynn hits differently. Before I can question myself, I turn in his arms and ghost my fingers over his injured collarbone, the thin scar peeking through the black ink that lines that shoulder and bicep.

"Stay," I whisper.

He does his best to remain unaffected by such a small plea, but I still notice the way he tenses for a split second.

"Stay, please." My voice is stronger, more determined when I ask again.

"Anything for you, sunshine."

Chapter 15
Drew

Did I intend on stepping into the shower with the love of my life today? Hell, no. I'm lucky she hasn't realized how much of a lovesick puppy I am. She could kick me to the curb every day for the rest of my life, and I'd still come crawling back, tail wagging and ready to try again.

The first time she whispers for me to stay, I can't stop the way my body freezes for a moment. No way did I hear her correctly. A figment of my imagination, surely.

But, no. When she says it again, it's damn near a command, one I'd be stupid to ignore.

As she backs her way to the shower, she slinks her hands under my shirt and pushes up. "I'd take it off, but I don't want to hurt you."

I help her slip it over my head and gingerly slide it off my injured side. Whether it's the shot from Doc Lindsey or the close proximity to a very naked Leila, I don't know, but the constant pulsing heat I usually feel is down to a low simmer. I'll take it.

Leila's eyes rake over me, her gaze burning a trail from abs to ink as her pointer finger instinctively traces the black lines. I know immediately when she spots the addition, hand freezing and breath sucking in.

I drop another kiss to her head before tuning her around. "Let's get in before all the hot water is gone."

"But your shorts."

"Don't matter."

"But you don't have clothes here." She tries to turn again as I step under the stream with her, the water at skin-melting temps. Leila melts as I pull her back to my chest, her mind and body finally giving in to the comfort I long to provide.

"I have a bag stashed in the hall closet," I whisper against her ear, causing goosebumps to spread down her arms.

"You gave me goosies," she whispers breathlessly, her head rolling back to look up at me. Oh, how I'd love to hear her like that in another situation.

I shift my hips back, trying to keep the bulge in my shorts from pressing into Leila's back, but she catches the movement. Before I can stop her, she shifts her hips to meet mine, a tiny moan escaping her lips as she succeeds in her mission to torture me.

Leila is quick. I barely catch her hand before it sneaks into my shorts, and the pout that takes over her face is enough to crack a smile on mine.

"This isn't about me, Gracie. No matter how much I've missed your touch. Now, tilt your head back so I can wet your hair."

She cuts her eyes at me, the pout turning into a scowl. "You don't have to wash my hair."

"Do you want me to stop?" I ask as my fingers begin massaging her scalp, her body becoming pliant in my hold. The pleasure sounds slipping from her throat have me questioning my resolve to keep this intimate moment innocent. "That's what I thought."

Leila remains quiet as I shampoo and condition her hair.

"Tilt back, baby," I rasp as I rinse the remaining suds and sift a comb through the strands. She's nearly asleep on her feet by the time I cut the water off and wrap her in the fluffy towel I'd already set out for her. Once she's wrapped like a burrito, I settle her on the closed toilet lid while I quickly dry off and hunt down my bag. Thankfully, Gavin and Kaia aren't back yet. The last thing I need is having to explain how settling Leila post-panic turned into a shower together.

Once I have both of us clothed—Leila in the shirt I'd discarded earlier at her request—I settle us both on the couch. The silence is comfortable, how it's always been with us. Leila curls into my side, her knees and feet tucked under my shirt.

"Why don't you get some sleep?" I suggest. "I know you didn't get any earlier, even if your brother thinks you were."

Instead of arguing with me, she leans into my side in a pseudo-hug and whispers that same four-letter word. "Stay."

I snag the blanket from the back of the couch and drape it over her before settling my arm around her and popping out the footrest. "Always, sunshine," I say as I place a kiss on her forehead. My words are met with soft snores as her body finally submits to the adrenaline crash. "You're stuck with me," I whisper.

Chapter 16
Leila

Both legs bounce against the console of Drew's truck as we pull into his parents' gravel driveway, anxiety coursing through my body at an alarming rate. It's weird. For some reason, it is unsettling to realize that the ranch house still looks the same as it did the last time I saw it. The white wraparound porch is pristine and accented with hanging plants, while a swing and rocking chairs occupy the larger corner. I used to love sitting out here, watching the sun set over the fields as the horses grazed. The sounds of town are distant, allowing nature's smaller critters to be heard.

Peace. Something I used to know. Something I long to find again.

The last time I saw any of them was right after everything went down with the deadbeats.

Decade-old memories don't soothe the tension in my gut. Some of it is residual from the panic attack earlier. While I was able to sleep off some of the weariness, I'm still a touch groggy. Drew tried to get me to reschedule this little get-together, if only until tomorrow, but I've already kept their granddaughter away for two months. Surely, there has to be some sort of animosity built up, even if his parents don't want to admit it.

Hell, I hate myself for not doing more. For not calling Drew more often. For not checking in on him after I found out about his accident. For not making sure he and his family were a part of Kaia's life from the beginning. Sure, I reached out a few times, but I could have tried harder. Could have called his mom or asked Kristen to tell him.

That's on me, and I'll have to live with the guilt that I deprived our daughter of the only grandparents she'll ever know.

"Breathe, Leila Grace." Drew's voice startles me enough to bring my focus back to the passenger seat of his truck. It's then I realize I'm gripping my seatbelt tight enough for my knuckles to turn white. His fingers gently pry mine loose before he wraps his much larger hand around mine and lifts it to press his lips along my knuckles. I suck in a breath at the intimacy but refuse to let myself shy away.

I said I was done running, and I meant it.

At least, I think I did.

I groan, my eyes closing as I lean back against the headrest. I'm borrowing panic from future situations. Therapy has at least taught me to recognize that much.

If I'm being honest with myself, I love the way he still treats me like I'm his without a second thought. It seems like it's second nature for Drew still, which makes me feel not quite so far out of my element. Because I still catch myself wanting to say and do things that aren't appropriate for us. Like staring at his ass as he walked away this morning, his Wranglers doing everything right in accenting his butt. He wasn't cursed with no-ass-at-all disease like most guys around here. And the backward ballcap with all his little curlycues sticking out from underneath? Geeze, you'd think I was still that little fourteen-year-old with a crush on her best friend.

Now, I'm just a twenty-six-year-old single mom with a crush on her baby daddy.

"Mom's excited to see Kaia again, and Dad is excited to meet her," Drew says, pulling me from my thought spiral. "But if at any point this starts to become too much, just say the word and we'll bounce. They'll understand."

I glance at the precious baby girl blowing bubbles in the back seat in the new car seat Drew must have had overnighted. She's more than content after getting all the snuggles and sunshine she could handle from Uncle Gavin. "This is a good thing. The right thing," I whisper, trying to convince myself as much as Drew.

He squeezes my hand again. "Just because something is *right* for one person, doesn't mean it's right for you, Leila."

Taking a deep breath to settle my nerves, I give his hand a small squeeze in return before opening my door and slipping out, the familiar feel of loose gravel crunching under my shoes.

Mrs. Flynn is on the porch before we make it to the steps. I fully expect her to snatch the infant carrier from Drew's hand, but she pulls me into her arms instead, squeezing me tight. We are nearly the same height, and it's instinctual to settle my head on her shoulder as I soak in the hug I desperately need.

"We've missed you so much, Leila Grace," she says, her voice cracking with emotion. It's almost too much, almost breaks my shields wide open.

"I'm so sorry," I mumble into her shoulder, but she strokes my back gently, soothing me like a child. Like her child.

"None of that, sweet child." She steps back, not-so-discreetly dabbing the corner of her eye. "Now, let's get that precious baby out of the heat so I can get some more snuggles while we wait on dinner to finish cooking," she says before ushering us into the house. The open floor plan allows Declan and Kristen to wave at us from their place by the screened back porch where the large red cedar picnic table still sits after all these years. I offer a tentative smile and wave, Drew's presence at my back the only thing keeping me from running for the door.

The next voice I hear nearly brings me to my knees, and I barely contain the sob that threatens to burst free at the sight of Drew's father. "Leila Grace Barrett, as I live and breathe."

He barely has the words out before I sling myself into his chest. While both of Drew's parents played an integral part in my upbringing, Mr. Flynn took on the "dad" roll when Gavin and I lost ours. He made sure to attend every school function, hauled the trailer to all of my brother's roping competitions, and made an appearance at every softball practice and game for the short time I thought I could be athletically inclined with anything that included a spherical object.

There's a reason I stick to running and boxing.

"Oh, how we've missed you, my girl."

"Yeah?"

"This house hasn't been the same since you left."

The little girl in me can't help but peek through my wet lashes. "You're not mad at me?"

He holds me at arm's length, a look of shock on his face. "Mad at you? Never, kiddo," he whispers before pulling me back into his arms and swaying us side to side. "You needed to get out of here, and that's exactly what your brother made happen."

"But Kaia—"

"Now, where is that precious granddaughter of mine?" he interrupts, and I can't help but feel giddy as his eyes light up at the prospect of meeting his first grandchild. "Is she ready for Yoo-Hoo in her bottle yet?"

Drew steps forward, at some point having removed Kaia from her carrier. She's nestled against his chest, knuckles in her mouth. "Not quite old enough, Dad. Give her a month or two before you traumatize Leila Grace."

I huff a laugh as Drew winks at me.

"I'll take baby girl to the back porch to see her aunt and uncle, if you're comfortable with that." He words it as a question, and I recognize it as the out he means it to be. His smile is gentle, reassuring as he steps forward and cradles my cheek in his palm. "I've got her. You two catch up. Holler if you need us."

As Drew and Mrs. Flynn slip into the living room, Mr. Flynn asks, "You hangin' in there, kiddo?"

My voice croaks as I attempt to push out words. Instead, I huff a breath as tears once again threaten to spill over.

He wraps his arms around me again, holding me the way only a loving father can. "You know, I've never been able to handle when my girls are hurting. Especially when it isn't something I can fix with baling twine or duct tape."

A choked laugh slips through my lips as I try my best to stop the emotional attack.

He rests his chin on my head, his voice a soothing presence. "The missus and I are so proud of you, Leila."

"Now you're just trying to turn me into a sobbing mess." I sniff, wiping under my eyes with the collar of my shirt.

"Nonsense. It's just truth you should have been made aware of a long time ago. We always hoped you would come back on your own volition. After what you endured here in this town, no one in this family—Drew included—wanted to guilt you into coming back here. You had every right to hightail it out of here and never look back. Instead, you're here, facing your demons head first." He steps back, cupping my face between calloused hands that have seen a lifetime of ranch work. "You are so brave, Leila Barrett. You brought a beautiful baby girl into this world with next to no support system and then put your own fears on the back burner to return to the town that caused them. But know this. No matter what happens, whether you and Drew find your way back to each other, whether you decide being in Havenwood is too much long-term, you will always be a daughter to us."

And cue the waterworks again.

"Sunshine? Everything okay?"

I turn at the sound of Drew's voice, intent on telling him that I'm fine. Instead, I take in the concern in his eyes and the reaching of his hand that he tries to stop. I should tell him nothing is wrong, assure him that I'm just emotional being back under the Flynns' roof.

And that's all true. I am fine, technically speaking. Our daughter is safe and very much loved.

I'm safe.

For the first time in years, I *feel* safe. Supported. Loved.

How do I put into words that I'm falling apart because the man who has been a father figure to me since the loss of my own just verbally claimed me as his daughter? That all my fears of being judged, of being shunned, ridiculed, hated for staying away were for naught.

That I have people in this world who love me.

Instead of voicing any of that, I turn from Mr. Flynn's hold and step into Drew's chest. His good arm wraps around me instinctively as I nuzzle my head into the base of his neck, the hand in the sling teasing the exposed skin of my bicep.

He presses his lips to my forehead before looking at his dad. "Didn't want to interrupt you two, but Mom needs you to help her with the potatoes. Something about making sure to not use whole a stick of butter this time?"

Mr. Flynn chuckles, the sound coming all the way from his belly. "Potatoes can never have too much butter. You'd think she'd know that after forty-three years of being with me. I make the best damn taters." His boots pad softly on the wood floor as he slips into the kitchen, leaving the me and Drew alone.

Drew's hand travels to my chin, forcing my eyes to meet his. "You sure this isn't too much, too soon?"

I shake my head even as another tear trickles down my cheek. "Swear I'm good," I whisper before tucking my head against his chest again. "Just missed this feeling."

He hums in understanding, though whether he thinks I'm referring to being in his parents' home or against his chest, I'm not sure.

He'd be right either way.

"Mom and Kristen are fighting over who gets to hold Kaia while you eat."

"And Declan?"

"He's snuggling her as we speak."

"I hate they never had any of their own."

His heavy sigh rocks our bodies. "They're finally coming to terms with it, I think. There's even talk of fostering since she has connections through her psychiatry and nursing background."

"They'd both be so good at it. Parenting kids with unkind pasts, I mean." After all, I feel like I have a pretty solid history as an example of how patient Kristen is with all of our sessions over the years. And the day everything changed between us notwithstanding, Declan has never once made me feel uncomfortable. Not even after the night I was attacked, when any man not Drew or my brother could trigger a panic attack.

We stand in silence, my head tucked under Drew's chin as he holds me close to his side. I melt into him, but I can still feel the tension radiating from his body.

"Your thoughts are begging to be let out, Andrew Malakai Flynn. Let 'em fly."

He chuckles, and some of the tightness in his muscles relaxes. "Just have something to ask you, but I have a feeling it'll be a longer conversation than we have time for right now."

As much as I want to press him for more, I know better. Drew has always been easy to read, but it's by his choice. He can close down and keep even the biggest secret tucked away when he wants.

"I guess it's a good thing you're staying over again tonight, then, isn't it?" I lean my head back, a soft smile—a real one—sliding onto my face. Maybe it's too bold, too forward for whatever this is that's stirring between us, but I'm trying to embrace what makes me happy.

"Yeah, sunshine," he says before pressing a gentle kiss to my forehead. "I guess it is."

And if this feeling of hope and love inside my chest is anything to go by, happiness won't be going anywhere.

"Come on, sunshine. Let's go face the music."

He wraps his arm around my shoulder, guiding me into the kitchen where I'm sure pretty much everyone could hear what was said. But no one acknowledges it. Kaia looks content snuggled into her uncle's chest, and the glassy look in his eyes makes me confident that she's wrapped another protective male around her tiny little fingers. I'll have to apologize to her in the years to come. *Good luck dating, baby girl.*

Kristen is the first to notice us, and she waltzes over, wrapping me in a hug.

Maybe it's weird having a friendship with my therapist, but I think that's the only reason I'm comfortable going to our sessions. Because she isn't a stranger trying to pry into the darkest recesses of my mind. Her petite frame and blonde hair always make me think of an ice princess, especially with those glacial-blue eyes of hers.

She lets go and brushes a loose strand of hair over my shoulder in a very motherly gesture, and I feel the guilt creeping in not for the first time. Here I am, a mother to a completely unplanned, healthy baby, and she's been trying to conceive and carry for years.

She catches the shift in my mood and smiles softly, her hand cradling the side of my head. "None of that," she whispers knowingly. Glancing up at Drew, she nods at his shoulder brace. "Hey, kid. How'd your visit with the doc go?"

"How it looks," he grumbles. "Not exactly rainbows and butterflies." He filled me in after my nap, that he's limited for several days. Not that it's stopped him from toting Kaia around.

Have you ever met a cowboy who wasn't stubborn to the bone?

Yeah, me neither.

Kristen's expression is sympathetic with understanding. She was a trauma nurse before changing professions and going back to school for psychiatry. She worked out of an Atlanta clinic for a while but finally opened her own practice here in Havenwood not too long ago. I'm pretty sure just about everyone in this town has gone to chat with her at least once. Just another way Havenwood is unlike any other town: everyone here promotes positive mental health alongside the physical.

"Well, come on. Find a seat," she says before looking up at Drew. "Now that your dad's added six pounds of butter to the potatoes—"

"And half the jar of salt," Declan chimes in, chuckling.

"—and more than enough sodium, we should be ready to eat."

Mrs. Flynn huffs in faked exasperation, her hands on her plump hips and a look of pure adoration on her face as she takes in the sight of all of us. "You'd think I raised you lot in a barn or something."

Mr. Flynn cuts in, setting the pot of mashed potatoes on an iron trivet. "I tried, honey, but you said that it would be frowned upon to leave them in the stalls overnight when they were throwing fits."

The whole table laughs as Mrs. Flynn rubs her brow and mumbles under her breath before swatting her dish towel at her husband. "I should've locked you in the barn a few times, too, mister. You caused just as much mayhem as these boys and Leila did."

I scoff, only slightly offended. "I did no such thing."

This time, it's Drew's turn to sound the exasperation. "Excuse me? Nine times out of ten, *you* were the reason I got in trouble."

I offer him a cheeky grin as I lean back against his chest. "Not my fault you always took the blame."

He huffs but hugs me to him before dropping a kiss to the top of my head.

I turn my focus to Kaia so I don't have to pay attention to the smug look on Drew's parents' faces. "Dec, I can take her."

He's already shaking his head before I can take a step forward. "Nope. You're gonna sit there and eat in peace while Mom and Kris take turns fawning over my perfect angel of a niece. Then I'm going to steal her back and show her around the ranch. We need to see what her breed and color preferences are so Dad can buy her a horse for Christmas."

"Declan," I huff.

He passes my baby girl to his wife before moving toward me, stopping a respectable distance away. I've known him since I was tiny, but he knows his size is a trigger. My stepfather used his size to intimidate me, so anyone over six-foot has the potential to kickstart an episode.

Drew starts to step in front of me, the beginnings of a growl slipping through his lips as his protective streak swims to the surface. "Don't start anything, brother. I love you, but I'll gladly knock you out if you hurt her feelings, shoulder be damned."

Declan shakes his head, palms up in surrender. Or maybe as a peace offering? "Apologizing, kid." He glances between the two of us. "We all made our own choices, but mine set all of this into motion."

I shift my weight forward with the intent of telling him not to apologize, but Drew's arm tightens around my waist, keeping me in place. Declan smiles, but the pain and guilt in his eyes is almost too much to witness.

"That night...all I heard was your scream. Every worst-case scenario slammed into me at that sound."

"Wait," I say. "You knew I was in your hotel suite?"

Drew's body shakes in silent laughter, and it takes everything in me not to stomp his toe like a little kid throwing a tantrum. As my eyes move back to Declan, I realize he's laughing quietly, too.

"You guys suck." I pout even as those pesky little tendrils of hope and love continue to weave and interconnect the broken pieces of my soul.

"You'd be a terrible spy, Leila Grace. Anyway, I reacted poorly when I found the two of you, you know…" He glances away, his cheeks tinging as pink as mine probably are at the reminder that he caught me and Drew in bed together. Naked. Post horizontal hokey pokey.

Drew leans down to whisper in my ear loud enough for his brother to hear. "Kind of enjoying his embarrassment, aren't you?"

This time, I do stomp his toe in warning, but a soft giggle slips through my lips. "You guys are nuts."

"Damn right, it was embarrassing. I saw your naked ass more than enough when we shared a bathroom," Declan shoots back before sobering. "Almost done, I swear. It was never my intention to force you guys apart. And then I made an ass of myself by assuming that you knew more than you did about Drew's accident and surgeries and still chose to stay away."

"Just wait until Doc gives me the all clear. You and me and the boxing ring," Drew grumbles.

I reach back, rubbing his arm in soothing motions.

"I'll give you a free shot," says Declan. "My wife has more than shown me the error of my ways, and your plate was more than full growing and birthing the most perfect addition to our family. So, I am profoundly sorry, to the both of you, for stepping in shit that was none of my business." He looks thoroughly chastised, even though he's the one offering the apology.

Drew looks dumbfounded, but their parents, and even Kristen, look pleased.

If I had to guess, this was part of why Mrs. Flynn called a family dinner. This kitchen has heard all of our ups and downs, all the good and bad of our youth. And now, our adulthood as well.

While family meals used to be weekly when we were kids—as in, it didn't matter what sports, school assignments, or social plans we had, everyone was expected at the table whenever family dinner was scheduled—Drew had told me years ago that they'd stopped having them as often once I left. Looking back, I wonder if we had them because they knew more about my homelife than they ever let on.

Probably.

By the time I was fourteen, I was sleeping over at least three nights a week. Drew's parents never asked if my mom knew where I was. Never questioned it when I showed up for dinner or if I was on the porch swing when Mr. Flynn headed to the barn as the sun came up.

Hell, most days, Drew even brought lunch to school for me. He was two grades ahead of me, but our high school only had one lunch period. We ate together on a bench in the school courtyard most days. Our own little oasis.

As my focus comes back to the meal on the table, I realize Drew has already started filling my plate before cutting the loin into bitesize pieces.

"I can cut my own food, you know."

"Mhmm. Or I can do it for you," he says as he passes it to me. "Eat up, sunshine. Give baby girl some tasty homemade southern comfort food in her next feed."

My cheeks heat at his casual mention of breastfeeding while a feeling of rightness and desire settle in my belly.

It's peaceful, eating dinner with this family. And when Mrs. Flynn brings out two homemade banana puddings, I'm done for. From-scratch banana pudding is far superior to any other dessert.

"This one is for you to take home, sweetheart." She motions to the one with foil over the top. "There's no merengue on it, extra wafers added after it baked, just like you prefer."

"You didn't need to do that." I sniff, dabbing the corner of my eye. "Swear you guys just want a waterworks show tonight."

"Nonsense. And tell that brother of yours he can't have any. He should've shown up for dinner if he wanted some."

A snort-laugh bubbles through the tears. Gavin decided to hang out with Kelsey tonight since they've both been busy with work.

Three servings of banana pudding later—don't judge, I haven't had any in a decade—Kaia starts to get fussy for the first time. A glance at the oven clock lets me know it's been almost three and a half hours since I last fed her. Drew is already scooping her into his arms and settling a pacifier between her lips before I can shift to my feet. "Did you pack a bottle or do you want me to occupy her until we head out so you can nurse at home?"

It's like acknowledging the time triggers my letdown, the heaviness in my breasts suddenly demanding to be nursed or pumped. Then I glance at the hopeful look on Drew's face, and it makes the decision easy. "The thermos with what I pumped earlier is in the insulated pocket of the diaper bag. The bottle is in the side pocket. I'll go handle this so you can feed her again later if you want," I add quietly, trying to keep the conversation between us.

"You sure? If you'd rather nurse, do it. I don't want you to be uncomfortable. Your weird boob contraption thing doesn't look too appealing. Looks more like some kind of nipple torture device."

I cover my face with both hands and groan as Kristen and Mrs. Flynn try to stifle their own laughter. This man is seriously discussing my breast pump at the dinner table in front of his dad and brother, who both look mortified, by the way.

"Go before I die of embarrassment," I say as I stand and drop a kiss to our beautiful daughter's dark curls before discreetly snagging my manual pump and pouch from my purse and disappearing to the front porch swing. My solace.

"What did I say?" he asks before I'm out of earshot.

"I need ear bleach," Mr. Flynn mumbles, which leads to the ladies finally giving in to their fits of laughter.

I can't help but laugh with them. Something about this house, this family, soothes the rough edges and further solidifies my desire to make the most out of this life and our circumstances.

***

Once I get my equipment and liquid gold and stored away, I step back into the house and risk a glance at the remaining family. I guess Declan followed Drew. Yeah, Kaia is definitely in for it when she gets her first crush.

Mr. Flynn is busy loading the dishwasher and divvying out leftovers, but both Mrs. Flynn and Kristen are watching me from the back porch.

"What?" I ask, suddenly embarrassed at being the sole focus of their attention. Yet, I still make my way to the rocker next to them.

Mrs. Flynn shakes her head, a sad smile taking over her thoughtful expression. "We just missed this. You." She reaches over, taking my hand in hers and giving it a gentle squeeze. "The two of you were always so good together."

I startle. "I'm not—I mean, we never..."

A soft giggle escapes Kristen as Mrs. Flynn tilts her head and lifts a brow. "Don't think you can pull one over on me, young lady. Mama knows all." Her lips quirk up at the corners, laugh lines prominent in the evening light. "The two of you were smitten from day one, and while I can understand why you tried to keep it from your brothers, the rest of us were never fooled. All those years of you tiptoeing in and out of his bedroom when you thought we were sleeping. No other girl ever had a chance at holding my baby's heart. We knew why Drew always demanded to tag along on those trips. That boy loves you, sweetheart. And it's more than obvious that he's head over boots for my precious granddaughter, too."

Kristen nods encouragingly when I look to her. "He was stressed to the max when he found out you were coming back, but since then, he's lighter. Freer than he's been since before the accident. He missed you. We all did."

I look down at my fingers as I fiddle with the hem of my shirt. "I keep telling myself I'm scared to let myself fall again."

"Honey, you've saved each other again and again, always pulled into the other's orbit. Even from a state away. Your relationship—friendship, whatever you want to call it—runs deeper than any other I've seen in my fifty-eight years on this Earth. To us, you are Leila Grace. To that boy in there rocking a tiny nugget when he'd never held a baby before last week? You are his world. His sunshine. His reason for fighting to put his demons to rest. Honey, you are his saving grace. And I really think, if you let him, that he can still be yours, too."

I sniff back the emotions that threaten to overtake me, but I still feel a tear trickle down my cheek. As much as I want to melt into those words, to believe every syllable, the doubts are still there. "But what if you're wrong? What if we aren't meant for more? What if we give this a shot, and it crashes and burns? We have Kaia to think about."

"And you'd both continue to put her first. But, Leila, think about it this way. Will your heart ever truly be happy if you never try? Wouldn't you rather give it a chance—give *him* a chance—before giving up your own happiness by never trying?"

They catch me up on the changes Havenwood has seen in recent years. Like Jace taking over the bar for his parents, how Jett and Noah ended up in partnership with Kelsey's bakery, and how there's talk of a single mom moving into the loft above the bar soon. By the time Drew slips back onto the porch with Kaia asleep on his chest, it's pushing ten o'clock.

"You about ready to head out, Gracie?"

I nod, mumbling an incoherent agreement. I want nothing more than to go home and sink into the covers with him and our baby girl cuddled close. Maybe turn on a movie and shut out the world like we used to as kids.

Yeah, that sounds like perfection.

***

By the time I settle Kaia into her crib for the night and cross all my fingers and toes that she sleeps past midnight, I quietly return to the living room, where Drew is kicked back on the couch with an episode of one of our old favorite shows playing quietly on the television. Gavin sent a text letting me know that he was going to crash at Kelsey's place. I'm still waiting on the day that they elope. They are perfect for each other, her happy optimism complimenting his grumpy seriousness. Maybe they'll figure it out one day.

Drew tosses his shoulder brace to the floor and pats the spot next to him. "Come, sit."

"Is that a good idea?" I ask, motioning to the black straps as they land haphazardly on the wood floor.

"I'll be careful."

Settling in next to him, I keep a small amount of space between us, but he nudges my knee with his and settles his arm around my shoulders. It's quiet between us, and I assume he's just focused on the show until he speaks.

"I'm tired of pretending, Leila Grace."

My shoulders tense as his words send my thoughts spiraling. *What could he mean? Pretending about being all in? Does he regret earlier? Or...or is he referring to us?*

Locking my thoughts down, I sit up a little straighter from where I'd allowed myself to settle into his side. "You shouldn't have to pretend about anything, Drew."

"Good. Glad you feel that way. Because you need to know."

"Know what? You're scaring me a little."

He turns to face me, taking my hands in his. "I need you to know, regardless of how you feel, I am all in. With Kaia, but also with you."

I start to push away, to stand and put more space between us, but he settles a hand on my thigh. Not restricting, just steadying. "Sunshine, please. My choices over the last year have been less than desirable, and I in no way deserve even a moment of your time. I will never be deserving of your heart, but I am in, one thousand percent. No matter what you decide."

"My heart can't handle any more fractures, Drew." My voice waivers as I realize how true that statement is. And yet, part of me is already all in, too.

"I never want to be the reason you cry anything other than happy tears for the rest of our lives, Leila Grace." He cradles my face between his calloused hands, and it makes me feel so small but so protected. Safe. Secure. His thumb pads away the moisture gathering under my eyes. "You and our little girl are my world. I know I don't deserve it, but I'm begging you to give us another chance. Not just for Kaia, because I know we would kick ass at co-parenting, but for us."

Taking a deep breath to settle my nerves, I nod. "You didn't let me finish," I whisper as I lean into his hand. I don't trust my voice or the ability to keep more tears at bay, but I let go anyway, letting my emotions shine through my eyes as happy tears continue to trickle down my face. Damn these hormone changes. Sighing and relaxing my shoulders, I finally glance back into Drew's deep-blue eyes and smile. "I can't handle more fractures, but I meant it earlier when I said I wanted to learn to live, to be brave. And I want to do it by your side."

The pure joy that fills his eyes is enough to make me giggle, even as he squeezes me to his chest. My hands settle on his forearms as contentment flows through me. Sure, fear of the unknown is still there, but I meant my words earlier and I mean them now. I'm done hiding. It's time to live.

"One more thing," Drew says, unwilling to meet my eyes. "But promise me you'll consider it before just shutting me down."

His tone is saturated in nervous energy, but he holds me tighter when I try to push away to get a better read on his face. Suddenly uncertain, I ask, "Drew, what did you do?"

"Don't panic."

Before I can complain about his poor word choice—because who tells a girl with a trauma-induced panic disorder not to panic—he sighs. "Just...I may or may not have purchased a small house a little over a year ago."

Chapter 17
Drew

The look on Leila Grace's face would be comical if it wasn't directed at me.

"I'm sorry. You what? When? What—"

When she pushes away from me this time, I let her go enough for her to look up at me but keep her close. The gears are turning, and I'm not sure I want to know her thoughts. But it's time to get everything in the open. If we are really giving ourselves another shot at a relationship, one not clouded by secrets and hiding, albeit poorly, from our families, then it's time to tell her.

"But you live above the gym. If you bought a house, why—"

"I bought the house for *us*. In the hopes that I could convince you to move back home. But then Declan caught us sneaking around, I let my pride win out, and then when I made plans to come back to you, everything fell apart.

"You bought a house."

I nod. "Yep."

"For us. Even though I was in a different state."

"I'd hoped to convince you. Gavin had said—"

"Whoa. Wait, what?"

Ah, shit. Leila pieces it together. I can literally *see* the puzzle pieces fitting in her mind.

"You're telling me that Gavin, my big brother, that tall broody overprotective grump of a man, *knew* you'd bought a house for *us*, but neither of you thought it needed mentioning? What the heck, Drew?"

I decide to keep it to myself that I was going to ask her to marry me. Maybe now isn't the best time. Besides, I didn't mean to throw Gavin under the bus. Sometimes my mouth moves faster than my brain.

"Wait. So, everyone knew about us except for Declan? And nobody bothered to say anything?"

"What do you mean by everyone? I only told Gavin because I wanted him to have a heads up."

"If Gavin knew, then Kelsey knew. And your mom and Kristen already confirmed that they all knew. Well, I guess I technically told Kristen, but I think she'd guessed it anyway."

So, Declan and Jace. That makes me feel like a shit friend. Instead of focusing on it, I push forward.

"I'm done hiding from this. From us. I've known since we were kids that you were it for me. No one else could ever make me feel the way you do, sunshine. You can argue it all you want," I say when she opens her mouth to do just that. "Tell me you're just in Havenwood for Kaia's sake. Tell me what we had all these years wasn't real, or that you don't feel the same way. That those moments in that hallway bathroom this afternoon meant nothing to you. But the truth is, if you say any of that, you'd be lying. And, Leila Grace, you are many, many glorious things, but a liar is not one of them."

Leila's eyes get that glassy sheen that says she's fighting for control over her emotions, wanting to lock down whatever she deems as weakness in this moment.

I want her to lay it all out there for me. Every fear. Every anxious thought. Every idea. Everything.

"So, yes. I bought a house for us. It's small, three bedrooms. Five acres on the backside of my parents' lot. It has a fenced yard and a porch swing that is perfect for watching the sun set. Already furnished and ready to go. We don't have to share a room, I can be there to help you with Kaia without risking my spine on this ancient thing Gavin calls a couch, and you can get out of Gavin's space like you wanted to."

She snorts a laugh, and damn did I miss that sound. "I'm not going to move out of Gavin's house just to burden you with the stress of living with an infant," she says. "I'm not saddling you with that kind of trouble."

"It isn't trouble when it's the two girls who matter most."

"I still have nightmares. Ugly ones that are...not fun. Especially when they wake Kaia."

"All the more reason to move in."

She's searching her brain for any possible reason to say no, so I keep pressing and hoping my luck doesn't run out.

"Move in with me," I beg. I am seconds away from dropping to my knees before her. "Gavin will be right down the road instead of down the hall. I get to spoil my girls 24-7." I slide the hand on her cheek over her shoulder and cradle her head, my fingers resting at the base of her neck. "Kaia gets both parents under the same roof."

I tug her closer, my forehead resting against hers, and I want nothing more than to lean forward and brush my lips across hers. But I know that'd be pushing my luck a little too far.

"And hopefully," I whisper. "Hopefully, I get to prove that I'm all in for the both of you."

"Drew," she says just as softly.

"If I thought you'd agree, I'd drag us both down to the courthouse first thing tomorrow morning and marry you."

"You don't know what you're asking," she says, the words almost sounding pained. As if she's forcing them out but doesn't fully believe them. Good. She should know by now that I am a man of my word. I know exactly what I'm asking of her.

"You let me be the judge of that, sunshine. I made the mistake of walking away once before. I won't let it happen again."

"I don't know what to say."

"Say okay."

She tries to look away from me, but this time, I do drop to my knees. Her eyes widen as she takes in the scenario.

"We've got this, sunshine. Let me prove it."

For a moment, I wonder if I judged this wrong. If she's going to kick me out and run back to Tennessee.

But then she huffs a breath and nods. "Okay."

My head shoots up, and I can't contain the grin that splits across my face. "Yeah?"

She nods, my smile clearly contagious. "But don't you dare drag me to the courthouse in the morning."

I stand, slipping my hands under her hair and cradling the back of her neck. "I'm going to kiss you now, Leila Grace Barrett," I whisper.

"Damn right, you're going to kiss me now," she says before pressing her lips to mine.

And for the first time in eleven months and twenty-seven days, all is right in my world.

Chapter 18
Leila

It feels like a dream, the good kind that I never want to wake from. The scents of sandalwood and something purely Drew wrap around me as snug as the arm across my chest. The satisfied sigh that slips out as I settle into the warmth at my back pulls a soft chuckle from Drew.

"Mornin', sunshine," he whispers with a kiss to my head and...

"Are you sniffing me?" I ask, a giggle bubbling up.

He sniffs my neck this time, purposely exaggerating the action. "Mhmm. Smells like summertime and heaven." The hand banded around my stomach starts to trail up my chest to cup my breast, reminding me of why I had to wake from the first sound night of sleep I've had in forever.

"As much as I'd love to let you do that, please don't."

Drew pulls his arm back, his hand resting on my side as I tilt my head to see him better.

"My boobs are about to explode," I whisper, another giggle covering the words as Drew's lips meet mine in a tender kiss. As he rolls to hover over me, I wrap my arms around his neck before hooking my leg around his hip.

Yep. These boobs are definitely about to explode.

As if he can read my thoughts—and let's be real: he probably can—Drew sighs, dropping his forehead to mine.

"Go feed the princess, sunshine. Then we can go grab a bite."

The trill of a ringtone cuts through the room, interrupting the intimacy of the moment. He answers, and something about the look on Drew's face as whatever the person on the other end of the line says registers puts me on edge.

"I'll be there soon. Just close off the entrance to the big field and make sure no one opens the gate closest to the barn until I get there," he says before ending the call and searching for his clothes.

"What happened?" I ask, already pulling clean clothes from the pile on top of my dresser.

"That was Gavin. Havoc is loose in one of the big fields and no one can catch him."

"Is he contained or literally running around an open field?"

"It's fenced. He's running the fence line, though. Probably trying to get back to his small paddock."

"Give me a few to get Kaia ready and to grab my pump."

"You don't have to—"

"He doesn't trust anyone, right? But he nuzzles me, lets me brush him. I understand being wary of people better than most, and he senses that. So, I'm going with you, cowboy."

"I love it when you're bossy."

***

When Drew's pickup finally rolls to a stop in front of the old red barn, Gavin and another guy who looks vaguely familiar are waiting for us.

"That's Reece, Jett's brother," Drew says as he puts the truck in park.

"One of the new guys put Havoc in the open field by the arena. He's freaked out, running the fence line, snorting and hollering. Won't come anywhere close to the gate."

"Does he have a halter on at least?"

Reece nods. "Yeah, by some miracle. With the way he bolted from the kid, I was sure he'd snap the leather."

Gavin steps forward, taking the infant carrier from me, a sleeping Kaia oblivious to the goings-on. "Kaia and I'll go hang in my office so we aren't a distraction. Just holler if you need me." As he heads deeper into the admin portion of the barn, Reece tosses a thumb over his shoulder. "What do you need from the guys?"

"Tell everyone to stay away from this area. No power tools. No four-wheelers."

"Will do."

As Reece disappears around the corner to pass the word along, I follow Drew's tense form through the main entrance into the barn.

"Stay back from Havoc unless I tell you to step in."

"I can handle myself around young horses, Drew."

Before I can blink, Drew spins around and grabs me by the hips, pressing my back firmly against a stall front, the metal hay door solid against my spine. When I glance up, my breath catches.

Scratch that. My lungs come to a full halt at the emotions swirling in Drew's deep-blue eyes. As his forehead drops to mine, a shaky breath slips from his lips. His good arm brackets my head while the other hand gently strums up and down my side.

"Hey," I whisper, my hand cupping his five o'clock shadow.

Drew's eyes are closed now, tension lines looking almost painful, but he hums his acknowledgment.

"Just want you to know, any other man would have gotten knee to the balls for grabbing me like that."

The huff of an exasperated laugh draws some of the tension from his shoulders.

Mission successful.

I weave my fingers into the curs at the base of his neck, the ones sticking out from under his hat, and tug. "Just because I've been away does not mean I've forgotten how to handle myself around young horses. I'm a big girl, Drew. I was born and raised in this barn, just like you."

"I know, sunshine. I do. It's just...Havoc."

"Me and Havoc are buddies, remember? You're the one who still owes him apologies."

He nods in defeat before dropping a kiss to my forehead and stepping back. "Let's go catch us a fiery red colt."

The next few minutes happen in such a flash that I'm struggling to wrap my head around it. One minute, we are both at the gate watching Havoc kick and whinny as his body shakes with nervous energy. Then whether he catches our scents or hears our approach, I don't know, but his entire body settles. The arched, bulging muscles in his neck seem to shrink by half as he takes to breathing heavily, his ears flicking back and forth. When the traumatized three-year-old takes steps in our direction, neck and back supple, ears forward, I say a prayer that Drew doesn't faint from the shock of it.

This horse just soothed something in Drew with the simple action of expressing his trust to the man who was certain he had ruined the timid redhead.

And when that same gelding gently bumps his head into Drew's outstretched hand?

Neither of us has dry eyes.

Drew clips the lead rope to Havoc's halter while stroking the soft skin of Havoc's muzzle. When Havoc lips at Drew's pocket in search of a peppermint, Drew glances at me through damp lashes.

"Not a word, sunshine," he mumbles as he pulls out three soft mints that Havoc immediately steals on our walk back into the barn.

We're almost home free, close enough that I have Havoc's stall open. Havoc walked like a champ from the field, past the arena, into the barn, and down the barn aisle without an issue.

Until a farmhand cranks up the old tractor at the other end of the barn.

It happens in less than ten seconds, but it feels like slow motion. Havoc rears and rocks his massive shoulder into Drew on the way up. The momentum slings Drew into the stall wall, knocking him off his feet, but the rope is looped around his hand. All my mind can conjure is Havoc coming back down on top of Drew. Or worse, giving into the instinct to run while Drew is still caught in the lead rope.

Fighting past the panic because it won't help anything, I do my best to keep my tone conversational. Deep breath in, deep breath out. "Didn't you learn at, like, three years old to not wrap a lead rope around your hand for reasons exactly like this?" I ask as I snag the quick release knot on the halter.

Thank God whoever put it on him tied it correctly.

Drew's blue eyes squint up at me as he tries to breathe through the pain and not finding my statement the slightest bit amusing. "Something like that," he groans.

As soon as the pressure on his poll releases, Havoc settles back onto all four hooves.

"Such a good boy." I spread my arms wide and step behind his shoulder, effectively corralling him into the stall before shutting and latching the door. "You too, Havoc."

"She's got jokes. I'm on the ground, and she's got jokes," Drew huffs to himself.

"Just trying to make sure you're still coherent, baby," I shoot back, checking him over for any visible injuries as my heart tries to come out my throat and drop into my stomach at the same time.

"I'm fi—"

"Don't you *dare* tell me you're fine right now, Andrew Malakai."

He winces, and a small part of me hopes it's from my words rather than the physical pain I know he feels right now. Taking a deep breath to settle the adrenaline that has finally made its appearance, I squat in front of Drew and tilt his chin until our eyes meet.

"Tell me what you need, cowboy."

"Vicodin," he shoots back without pause.

"Ha! Funny guy."

His lips quirk up just enough to ease the vise around my heart. "A little funny. A little serious."

I groan at his ability to joke in the face of pain. "I need to know what to do here, Drew.

Seriously. Do I call 911? Drive you to the closest hospital? What?"

"Is taking me home and giving me a sponge bath a viable option?"

An undignified squeak flies out, and I'm not sorry for swatting at his uninjured side in disbelief at his misplaced humor. Even if the image does make me want to...

You know what? Not the time nor the point.

"It isn't even ten in the morning. Can you please take pity on my post-partum hormones and give me a straight answer?"

Drew tucks a loose hair behind my ear before cradling my jaw, the callouses on his palm helping to ground me as I fight off the budding panic. It's funny (not really) how I can get through an emergency, but the result is usually a full-on freakout breakdown moment.

"I can get to the truck. Get Kaia and drive us to my parents' house. We'll call Kristen and let her put that old trauma nurse experience to good use." He grunts in discomfort as he shifts to his knees before standing and offering me a hand. I ignore it, pushing myself to my feet before folding myself into Drew's chest.

"You swore you'd do what it takes to stay healthy. You won't let the doctor do the surgery you need. And you want me to brush this under the rug like you didn't just get slammed by a thousand-plus-pound hooved animal and joke about pain meds," I say, my voice getting more and more heated as I talk. Stepping out of his arms, I cross mine under my too-full breasts as I let the anger and fear mingle.

Drew is apparently triggered by this line of conversation as well. His already tall frame stretches up. I'm pretty sure he'd square his shoulders at me if it wouldn't make the situation physically worse for himself.

"Don't accuse me without the facts, Leila Grace," he says, his tone low and gravely. "I have been one hundred percent clean and sober for *months*. It'd have been a hell of a lot sooner had I known about Kaia."

I should walk away right now. Go get Gavin from his office or hunt down Reece or Declan. We should wait until both of us have a few minutes to breathe and think rationally, but we are nothing if not stubborn.

"No. Don't you dare bring our daughter into this," I snap. "I need to be able to trust you. If this is too much, if you're going to try to use Kaia to justify or excuse your actions, tell me now. I refuse to be responsible for putting you in a position that threatens your healing."

Drew almost looks stricken before steeling himself and locking down his emotions. "But that's exactly what you did, isn't it, Leila? You showed up, with our *daughter*, knowing damn well I didn't have a clue—"

"I didn't know you never listened to my messages," I interject.

"Then you must have even less faith in me than I'd thought. You honestly think I would have stayed away if I'd known I had a daughter? That I wouldn't have stepped up?"

The silence is tense, growing more and more so by the second. Even Havoc has quieted in his stall, choosing to stand as far from us as he can.

I want to take it back, erase the last ten minutes—hell, the last two hours—and put him at ease. But it means more than that to me. *He* means more than that to me.

I refuse to let a lack of communication ever come between us again. Instead of storming off, instead of slinging my worries in his face, I pause. It's a moment of growth. Instead of hiding behind the walls I've built, I let them all come crumbling down as every vulnerability shines through.

"I'm terrified of losing you again, Drew."

A crack in his armor finally shows as his chin dips to his chest and he opens his arms in offering. I gladly let his strength surround me, thankful he isn't letting this argument drive a wedge too deep.

"What do you say we get Kaia, go to my parents' house, and I let Kristen be the judge of what to do next?"

I nod, melting back into his embrace and accepting the compromise for the peace offering it is. "I can live with that."

Chapter 19
Drew

First of the month feed bills always cause my insides to cramp. October is the worst of them, though. It isn't because we can't afford it. The ranch does well, even with the limited training spots. But feeding twenty-plus head of twelve-hundred-pound animals as we prep for the winter months while battling soaked fields that resemble pig pens instead of hay fields and green pastures? It's overwhelming, to say the least.

I am not a numbers guy. Not a business man, either. I prefer manual labor, the physical strain it puts on the body. I love the burn that funnels through my muscles after a young horse tests the boundaries, both mine and his. The feel of leather between my fingers, feeling for every twitch, every ounce of tension that might indicate whether that horse will choose fight or flight.

That's why this pencil-pusher stuff is Gavin's job. He's amazing at it, always has been. It's why Dad hired him when he was still in high school. No one can keep this place organized as well as Gavin Barrett. And yet, I'm still doing monthly inventory because we—meaning Declan—neglected the record-tracking aspect. Kind of difficult to know how much feed and hay is needed if there isn't an updated record of how many horses eat how much. It's the curse of doing everything by memory—no one else can do the job.

A knock on the open barn office door pulls my focus away from the computer screen. Reece Taylor's head and shoulders lean around the door frame. He's been absent for most of the summer, having taken off to Kentucky to help his dad out, but the guy's been a solid farmhand and friend for the better part of the last five years.

"What's up, Reece?"

"Hey, man. Need you to head over to the gym. Jace tried to call you, but it went to voicemail."

I tap my phone screen and find three missed calls from my best friend. "Guess I still had it on silent. What's up?" I'm already up and shutting down the computer before he says another word. But when he does? It's like everything in me freezes and speeds up at the same time.

"Your girlfriend is beating down the heavyweight bag like a pro. Been at it for almost half an hour." I'm out the door before I realize it, jogging toward my truck with Reece on my heels as he continues to talk. "The guys thought she was just putting in a hard workout until Jace came in. He says he thinks she's stuck in—"

"—a panic attack. Yeah. Thanks for the heads up," I say as I slam my truck door with more force than necessary.

I drive the short distance to the gym, glad for the lack of speed traps, because I'm definitely in super speeder territory for our little residential town. As I step into the gym in a record three minutes, it is immediately apparent where Leila is. Also apparent is that there are too many busybodies in this town who don't know how to mind their own damn business.

"If you aren't working out, get out," I holler before stepping closer to Leila Grace, taking in her sweat-soaked shirt and loose hair.

She never boxes with her hair down.

As the bodies of the town nosey asses disperse, I study Leila's movements.

Leila generally has one of two reactions to a panic attack. The more common reaction is when her breathing becomes labored, heart pounding, vision blurs. If she doesn't do it on her own, someone usually guides her to the ground and helps her place her head between her knees while trying different grounding techniques.

The other reaction, the one I've only witnessed once before, is like she's physically fighting the panic.

It isn't obvious at first glance; Leila throws punch after punch into the bag, never flinching at the contact even as it sways unsteadily. No wonder no one else noticed it. But watching her more closely, I notice the vacant look in Leila's eyes. The bare fists and the uncontrolled pattern from her dominant hand give away her building panic.

Stepping up to Jace as he watches her with pain-filled eyes, I try to determine the best way to handle this. The last thing I want is for her to shut down after we've made so much progress. Maybe it's residual from that night forever ago when Declan caught us together in the middle of a panic attack, but I feel like my reaction to one of any kind could kick us right back to that hotel room. And I doubt we'd be so lucky as to survive unscathed and heal from that nightmare a second time.

"I tried talking to her. Was worried touching her would make things worse," Jace says, gesturing to his giant frame. Everyone who was around ten years ago remembers how massive Leila's stepfather was. The piece of trash deadbeat.

"Probably for the best. Depending on what triggered this one, your size might have made it worse."

Slowly, I move toward her, like approaching an untouched colt. "Leila," I call gently.

Her fists never slow as she punches with no regard for herself. Pure emotion—pure adrenaline—powers her swings. An occasional grunt or harsh breath are her only sounds as I call her name again.

I'm right on her without her awareness, waiting just outside her swing radius before touching my hand to her shoulder. I am fully prepared for the fist that swings around and lands in my palm. Her entire body seizes at the contact, shoulders drawing up, breath catching in her lungs. Her focus is zeroed in on our hands, but her eyes are vacant, trapped in her memories.

I've been present for more than a few of her panic attacks over the years, though none were in public. Glancing around, I ensure no one is sticking their nose where it doesn't belong before turning complete focus back to the girl in my arms.

Slowly, so as not to startle her while at the same time hoping to bring her back, I cup her cheek and lean down to rest my forehead against hers. "What's goin' through your mind, sunshine?"

Her lower lip quivers as a single tear slides down her cheek. I wipe it away with the pad of my thumb before pulling her tight to my chest, rubbing small circles along her spine, willing her to let me in.

The deep sigh mixed with a choked sob has me bringing her in closer for a squeeze before guiding her to the door. "Let's get out of here and clean up those split knuckles. Then we can see about some pizza and strawberry ice cream."

I maneuver her into my truck before leaning over her to secure the seatbelt. Her hands shake as they grip her thighs, breaths still more shallow than I'd like. As safely as I can, I rush us to the little house behind my parents' place.

This isn't how I'd planned on introducing her to this place. I'd hoped to take her to dinner then slowly make our way from room to room as she pointed out all the changes she'd make. Instead, Leila doesn't acknowledge the wraparound porch, the yellow rocking chairs, or the baby swing.

As I lead her through the front door and into the kitchen, she settles on one of the stools by the counter. I set about pulling my first aid supplies from the cabinet above the sink before making my way back over to her, thankful that I'd finally moved in over the weekend.

When she turns her head to avoid looking at me, I squat down until I'm in her line of sight. "You feel like talkin' about whatever just happened?" I dab the alcohol wipe along her knuckles, cleaning the specks of blood away. The quick flinch of her hand as the wipe does its job is the only indication she's still here with me, her gaze fixed on the scrapes that are sure to bruise.

One of her shoulders eventually shrugs to her ear as she glances away again. "Just needed to burn off some energy. It's fine. I'm fine." When she finally meets my gaze again, her beautiful eyes are dull, as void of emotion as her voice.

As I smear ointment over her knuckles, I say, "You're still a terrible liar, Leila Grace. When you want to give honesty a go, let me know." I do my best to keep the sound of frustration out of my tone, but some of it still slips in. I have no right to the feeling. She has no obligation to share anything with me. I'm beyond lucky that she shares our daughter.

We've finally started to get our lives back on track, and here she is shutting me out all over again. She's better than this, stronger than this, and every part of me wants her to admit that things are in fact *not* okay.

I sigh, crossing my arms and leaning my hip against the counter. She stares, her facial expression stoic.

At least she's looking at me.

Frustration simmers under my skin, but I refuse to acknowledge it, shoving it down and softening my voice. "You don't have to tell me what's up, but own up to not being okay. There's no shame in it. We've all got shit tearin' us up."

When her shoulders hunch forward and her chin dips to her chest, I've had enough. I'm not mad at Leila. Never at her.

No, I'm angry at the trauma she still faces day in and day out.

"Look at me, Leila," I say, voice as gentle as I can make it. "Let me see that sun shine through your eyes."

As misty eyes meet mine, Leila finally takes in a deep breath. It isn't as steady as I'd like, but it's progress.

"Atta girl, Gracie. Keep breathing for me. Just like that."

Chapter 20
Leila

I fight with myself as Drew continues staring at me, my inner demons screaming louder than common sense. His gaze burns through me, seeing past all the walls I've built over the years. The nightmares, the panic attacks, the dream chasing, the hopes and fears. He's been there through it all until the last year. He knows me on a level no one else ever could.

"Leila," he calls again, a little push of dominance in his tone, his posture widening.

I glance up cautiously, wrapping my arms around myself.

"Say it out loud, sunshine." His voice is softer now, almost a whisper. His body inches closer, forehead almost to mine.

"Tell me you aren't okay, and I will do everything in my power to make it better."

I shake my head. "I'm not," I whisper, nearly inaudible.

"What was that?" he asks. "I can't hear you."

"I am not okay," I mumble a little louder, pinpricks in my eyes threatening to unleash even more tears after I'd just dried the last round. Those four words create the most terrifying sentence I've uttered since becoming a mother.

"Own it, Leila." His body now looms over me, determination and something like adoration filling his gaze.

That look breaks through the splintering walls I've kept up since coming back to Havenwood. I push off the stool with enough force that it slams against the underside of the counter. My hands shove into Drew's chest, willing and ready to shove him back as well as I cry out in frustration.

"I'm not okay, okay? I. Am. Broken. I haven't slept in months. My own daughter would rather snuggle up with her uncle than with me unless it's to eat. And I apparently still can't walk past my stepdad's old house without triggering a stupid panic attack." I huff a few breaths as I get that off my chest. The new round of tears finally wins when I look up into those midnight-blue eyes as they overflow with compassion. "I'm not okay, Drew," I whisper, my chin quivering.

His long, calloused fingers grip my chin gently. "No, you aren't. And that is perfectly okay." Drew's thumb swipes up, ridding my face of tears. He never takes his eyes off of mine. In that moment, all of my fears, all the anxiety, disappear. There are no thoughts. Just instinct as I reach up on tiptoes and close the small distance between us, my lips finding his like they always used to.

To his credit, Drew doesn't hesitate or shy away, immediately taking control of the kiss. His lips are soft, the pressure just firm enough, slightly parted as his tongue darts out to swipe along my lower lip. I fall into the sensation of being held by the only man I've ever loved. The only one I've ever had an emotional connection with.

My hands travel around his back, caressing the muscles there as they play under my fingertips. I'm careful to avoid the material of the brace that's holding his left arm steady. Instead, I drop my fingers to the hem of his shirt and caress the skin just above his belt.

He groans and takes a step back, hands still gripping my hips. "Easy, Gracie."

I shudder at the sound of the old nickname on his lips but drop my hands, his words striking through my unusual carelessness. I tuck a section of hair behind my ear and take a step backward, suddenly unable to look at the man I'd just been lip-locked with.

"Don't do that," he says, pulling me back to him so we nearly touch front to front.

"Do what?"

"Shut down on me." He slips one hand around to rest on my lower back. "I'm trying my damnedest to remain a gentleman here, but I forgot how complicated you can make that."

My cheeks flare at his words.

A cheeky grin tugs at Drew's lips as he finally steps back and readjusts himself. "You're cute when you blush."

Tucking my chin, I don't know what to say, so I change the subject. "I need to go pick up Kaia. Gavin's been watching her for me today since my feelings felt too big for my body. Felt like my skin was going to split open for the world to see."

"Pretty sure that's who's been blowing up my phone."

"What?"

"Yeah, it's been vibrating in my back pocket for the last few minutes."

I groan as I run a hand roughly over my face while Drew answers his phone.

"Hey, man...No, she's with me. We're headed that way in just a few minutes...See you then." He hangs up and sets the phone on the counter.

Those blue orbs study me as if he can see straight through me. When I still don't say anything, he sighs, settling against the counter with his arms crossed over his chest. The move pulls his shirt tight, his ink peeking out from under the sleeves.

"Leila Grace Barrett, you are the most beautiful, patient, big-hearted woman I have ever met. You're compassionate, considerate, and overall, just one of the most amazing people I know." He steps forward, cradling my head in his hand. "But do you have to be the most stubborn person in this entire town?" His grip slides to the back of my head as he gently pulls me to his chest.

"I think that award goes to you," I whisper, my voice breaking slightly. Giving in to the security of his hold, I settle my ear over Drew's heartbeat, letting the sound ground me. Letting the feel of his arm, the strength in his grip, keep me in the present instead of where I'd been before Drew found me.

"I hope the day comes where you trust me enough to share whatever's going through your mind like you used to," he whispers just as softly, the tone a little raspier than normal as emotion consumes him, too.

Leaning back in shock, I take in his expression and realize he's dead serious. My fingers glide up his chest, running along the edges of the straps that sit there. "Oh, Drew. No, babe." The endearment slips out, but I don't let myself analyze it. "You are everything and more. I've been handling so much of this fear, this guilt, by myself for so long that I forget there's more than just me. It's more than a little terrifying voicing these things out loud. I know you're willing to listen, it's just..." The words get stuck as I try to ease his worries. The last thing I want him to think is that I don't trust him. Because this man is everything to me, and I'm quickly realizing there's no more pretending that I'm not in love with Drew.

With that realization, I smile.

Drew smiles back, but his eyes crinkle in confusion. "What are you smiling at, sunshine?"

"I'm in."

"You're...in?"

I nod, a giggle slipping free. "You gonna show me around, or what? I mean, assuming you didn't bring me to a stranger's house."

Understanding finally clicks. "You're in. As in, moving in?"

A grin consumes my face as I nod, despite the exhaustion and fogginess that pulls at my mind. "You going to show me around our new home or what?"

Chapter 21
Leila

"Are you sure you're okay with Kaia hanging out for a few hours? I can see if Kelsey minds watching her."

Kristen tsks at me as she plucks a bright-eyed Kaia from my arms. "Tell Mommy to have fun with Daddy, sweet girl. You and Aunt KK have chaos to cause this morning."

I choke on a laugh. "Please tell me you're good with this, again."

She tucks my daughter to her chest, the gentlest of smiles gracing her lips. "I have your number on speed dial. You have mine. Declan knows which trail you guys are taking if he needs to ride out to find you for any reason. We're just unboxing the nursery for you this morning, and Gavin will swing by later to help move some of the heavier stuff around. Go have fun. You and Drew both deserve the break."

"Thanks, Kristen."

"Now go before he sends out a search party for you."

***

I haven't been on a horse in so many years that I almost laughed in Drew's face when he suggested we hit the trails this morning. Not only am I exhausted from packing all my belongings into Drew's truck last night, but Kaia's poor little tummy has been tight and gassy since we started adding formula to her feeding routine. While he was prepping my coffee earlier, I not so subtly questioned his sanity for suggesting I sit on a twelve-hundred-pound animal when I haven't had more than four hours of sleep.

Now, as I watch him sling a pad and a saddle over the little chestnut gelding's back, I nearly have to bite my knuckle to keep the appreciative sound in. Apparently, I don't silence it too well. Drew glances over, his backward ballcap sitting low on his brows. It's well before midday, and his shirt already sports sweat marks from the hours he's been out here riding. When he slipped out of the house this morning with a quick kiss before the sun came up, I knew he was hoping to get some training rides in before the humidity skyrocketed again. I watch for any indication that his shoulder isn't up to this, but he's a grown man. I try my best to keep out of his way, even if worry eats away at me that he's overdoing it.

"Like what you see, sunshine?"

"You have no business looking that good when you're that filthy," I say before slapping a hand over my mouth in shock. I can't believe I said that.

I mean, it's true…but still.

He opens his arms and starts walking toward me, a dangerous smirk on his lips. One I recognize all too well.

"Don't you dare," I warn, backing away as quickly as I can without stumbling over the loose gravel.

"Oh, come on, sunshine. Don't you want a hug?"

Drew shoots forward, grabbing me as I squeal. His arms wrap around me, tucking me into his chest and rocking us side to side as I submit to the sweaty bear hug. His breath tickles my ear, settling something in me as we just sway. I hadn't realized the tension building in my chest until now.

"If you'd rather watch or just hang out and groom one of the mares, we can do that instead," Drew says, taking the tension as nerves about riding. Honestly, I can't pinpoint where the anxious energy is coming from. It's frustrating when there isn't a noticeable trigger.

"I want to ride I...I haven't been on since my dad died. Guess I'm just getting stuck in old feelings," I say, realizing thoughts of my dad are exactly what has me on edge.

"Wanna talk about it?" he asks as he goes back to readying the horses for us.

I study his nimble fingers as they manipulate the leather straps and buckles on the bridle, working off muscle memory. He doesn't even have to glance under the gelding's head. My treacherous thoughts can't help but slip to other ways those fingers could—

Drew's rumbling laugh interrupts my imagination. "Penny for whatever thought just went through your head, sunshine? It seems interesting from here."

I huff an irritated breath as I realize his eyes are firmly on me, a knowing glint in them. Yep, even my thoughts aren't safe from this man. And, apparently, I'm still a lovesick teenager with wild fantasies about the cowboy down the road.

Clearing my throat, I focus on the two horses in the crossties, effectively shifting our focus back to appropriate—safe—topics. "So, who are the two lucky lads who get to tote us today?"

Drew pats the neck of the bay colt closest to him. "This little stud is Loki, and I pray he doesn't decide to live up to his name today. The little red guy is just called Red. He's actually

Declan's, but he doesn't ride this one. Says he's too mellow so he just spoils him with too many peppermints instead."

I quirk an eyebrow at him. "He does? Or you do," I ask, nodding to the peppermint wrapper sticking out of his pocket.

"Definitely him," he says, stuffing the paper deeper. He tightens the girth on Red one more time before unhooking both horses and leading them toward the trail head. "You ready?"

"Yep. Just like riding a bike, right?"

***

Can confirm: horseback riding is *not* just like riding a bike. Sure, we've kept this little adventure to a walk—well, I have; Drew's little colt has pranced, jigged, and moonwalked down the path—but my thighs and tailbone are feeling every hoofbeat by the time we circle around the arena. We've mostly ridden in steady silence or Drew's guidance on how to maneuver Red down the trickier parts of the trail. His question from earlier still lingers, though, and I finally find the courage to answer it.

"You asked earlier if I wanted to talk about it...about Dad."

Drew looks over his shoulder at me, his hands and seat steady even as Loki goes on another sideways shuffle. "You guys just don't mention him much."

I shrug, suddenly finding interest in the tooling on the saddle horn. "He had that big black mare, the one with the blaze on her face and two white stockings."

"Delilah," he says softly, his voice carrying in the afternoon quiet.

"Yeah. He'd pony her off whatever gelding he had at the time, and I'd bounce around on her, all grins and giggles. That mare even let me use her neck as a slide. I begged my mother to let me keep her, but she laughed. Thought it was ridiculous to keep a thousand-pound animal around when she could sell it to fund her habits."

Red's ears flick side to side as his body tenses underneath me, and I realize my legs are gripping his sides with the rise in my own anxiety.

Breathing deep and exhaling through my mouth, I force my muscles to relax while scratching the sweet gelding's neck with my rein hand. "Sorry, bud," I whisper.

"She's living her best life as a retired broodmare in Kentucky."

My eyes snap up to Drew. "What? But she was sold to some backyard cowboy."

"Who my dad then threatened before paying double for her. He sent her to a friend's breeding farm just north of Lexington to keep your mom from knowing. They fell in love with her, bred her twice. Now, she's a glorified pasture pet that the grandkids ride bareback around the yard."

I'm not ready for the emotion that takes hold of me, the tears of gratitude that fill my eyes. "But...why?"

"Your dad was one of the good ones, Leila. Anyone with half a brain cell could see how much he loved you, your brother, and that horse. So, making sure all three of you were safe was the only thing that mattered," he says softly.

As I blink away the moisture, I realize we've both come to a stop at a small opening that overlooks the little town where a happy-go-lucky, horse-loving girl thrived. The town my dad loved more than anywhere else. Long-forgotten words he used to say fill my thoughts as I watch the quiet streets at the bottom of the hill.

This place'll be your saving grace, honey bee. Just you wait.

The hardest part of riding is the ground. Just like life. Live it up, Gracie girl.

I've long since given up on stopping the tears that roll down both of my cheeks, not bothering to wipe them. Without another thought, I slip my reins into the other hand and reach for Drew's. He takes my hand in his without question, without looking at me. As I glance at his face, I realize his eyes are misty as well.

"Both our dads always knew, didn't they? That we'd end up here."

Drew chuckles. "I doubt they knew we'd end up with a daughter before we got married."

I shove him gently, but my lips tug up at his jesting. Loki finally settles next to Red, as if he realizes the weight of this moment, these words.

As he relaxes with a full-body sigh, Drew runs a gentle hand along the colt's black mane, murmuring praise and assurance. "Yeah, Leila Grace. I think we're exactly where they wanted us to end up."

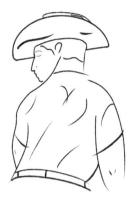

Epilogue – Drew

If you'd told me eighteen months ago that I'd be sitting in a box at Steele Arena with Leila on my lap and our nine-month-old, blue-eyed beauty of a daughter sitting across the room with her "Aunt KK" after a six-month shoulder rehab that has vastly improved my quality of life, I'd have laughed in your face. Because eighteen months ago, I chose pride over the love of my life, missed the pregnancy and birth of our baby girl, and would have rather set my shoulder on fire than undergo another procedure.

All those moments, all those missed opportunities, the toll of those physical, mental, and emotional struggles led us here.

Steele Valley's pro hockey team made it to the playoffs for the first time in franchise history, and since Noah is best friends with the team's starting center, our entire family is here to show our support. The neon, glitter-covered signs Oakley and Jett made are bright enough to blind the players if the lighting catches it just right.

"Did you know they call the puck a biscuit and the net a cage? Who comes up with this stuff?" Lelia asks as she studies an article on her phone. I'll keep to myself how adorable I find her when she doesn't understand something. "I mean, I'm all for supporting Silas and Oakley, and it's super impressive the team made it this far, but *why* would anyone want a tiny piece of rubber flying toward them at those speeds? And then, they skate closer! Are they all short a few screws?"

The chuckle that rumbles through my chest is drowned out by Jett and Noah's outright laughter. The two of them bleed Voltage red and black year-round, and today they're wearing team sweatshirts with Silas's number 31 on the back.

I give Leila's thigh a little squeeze as she continues to scroll through random hockey articles. "Definitely a special breed, but you've got to admit it's entertaining to watch. The adrenaline. The testosterone. It's almost tangible in this kind of environment," I say as my gaze once again shifts to the other side of the room.

Kaia stuffs another cheese puff into her little chipmunk cheeks while pointing and grabbing at all the snacks her precious little heart desires.

As I turn my focus back to the beautiful mama in my arms, Leila's green eyes cut through her lashes, faked annoyance sparkling in her eyes. "Of course, you think so. That's such a sports guy response."

"Oh, like you and Jett aren't sitting here imagining it's one of your hockey love story books?"

Jett snorts, nearly spilling her Dr.Pepper in the process. "Hey, now. You don't know good hockey romance until you've read the bad ones. This right here?" She motions to the ice where players are warming up. "This is real hockey romance. The sport needs to be engrained in the story. 'Reformed puck bunny and the coach' is one of my favorites. Plenty of angst, intimacy, and ice time."

I catch the subtle nudge Jett sends into Leila's arm before she pulls typical Jett antics. "Oooh, mama. Check out that hunk stretching right down there. Oh, wait. That's Silas. Hey, Oaks!" She leans around Noah, purposely pushing his head down to clear her line of sight. "Your boy toy is doing his sexy stretches! Hurry or you'll miss it!"

Noah gently moves his girlfriend back into her seat with an exasperated sigh. "Do you have to cause chaos where my sister is involved? I don't need those images in my head."

Jett shrugs, but the mischievous grin on her face says she knows exactly what pot she's stirring. "You're the one who told me to embrace the chaos, honey. Bet you regret it now, don't you?"

"Never, baby girl," he whispers before pressing a chaste kiss to her lips.

Jett chases his lips before the figurative switch in her head flips again and she spins back to Leila. "Speaking of baby girls and boy toys. Have you told him yet?" she asks excitedly.

Leila freezes in my arms, the struggle to not look at me evident when I lean around to catch a glimpse of her face.

Noah pulls Jett to her feet before guiding her to the snack table. "Okay, pretty girl. Time to remove yourself from this conversation before your foot lodges itself in your throat."

From my periphery, I can see Jett looking between us and Noah, confused, before Noah steers her away.

Yeah, so am I. My mind whirls over what Jett said, wanting to believe what I think it means but hesitant to hope.

"Sunshine?" I ask, guiding her eyes to mine with a finger to her chin.

Her breath catches as she finally looks at me. "How do you feel about having to buy diapers for several years to come?"

I graze my palm over her stomach almost teasingly, still needing her to say it outright. "Are you..."

When she settles both her hands over mine and gives me a watery smile, I'm done for. "We're pregnant," she whispers.

The shout of excitement slips out before I can even consider stopping it. I stand, pulling Leila into my arms and spinning her around. Everyone's eyes are on us, but I don't care. I only have eyes for the girl of my dreams. "Kaia gets to be a big sister," I whisper, amazement lining my voice as I shift my gaze to Leila's belly, my hands cradling it gently as I drop to my knees.

"You're making my insides all melty, Drew Flynn."

I glance up at her, ignoring the moisture gathering in my lashes. "I'll be there every step of the way this time. Swear it."

"I know you will, baby. Never doubted you."

Have you read Jett and Noah's story?

F ind it here:

https://www.amazon.com/dp/B0D8HLH4Y3

Turn the page to read the first chapter.

Chapter 1

"Come on, come on, come on," I mumble as I wait for this slow-as-molasses elevator. The temptation to press the call button again is almost too much.

My therapy appointment is in less than five minutes, and I look like a wet dog standing in the lobby of this Atlanta high rise. I should have stayed in bed. This is my punishment for thinking traffic would have died down by ten in the morning.

It didn't.

I even woke up early thanks to the rumbling of thunder shaking the house. Although, the being-ahead-of-schedule thing may have been the problem. False sense of security and all. I thought I had enough time to fix breakfast, so I threw together eggs, sausage, and a piece of toast.

It turns out reading while I cook and eat is a bad idea. I got lost in the pages of Siena Trap's most recent hockey romance and forgot I had to leave the house. Then the I-285 connector was a nightmare, because no one knows how to drive in the rain.

Again, I should have expected it. I'm a Georgia girl, through and through.

When I finally arrived at my therapist's office, the parking lot was full, so I had to park four blocks away and run to the building.

In the rain.

Without an umbrella.

Because why would I remember to grab the one I set by the door last night after checking the weather three times? Total craziness, I know.

And now this elevator is moving slower than a dial-up connection.

I sigh in relief as a ding finally signals the elevator's arrival and the light on the call button turns off. I rush through the doors as soon as they open, turning and pressing the twenty-seven and then spamming the close button, all while cursing McKenna for forcing me to schedule this appointment for today. Groaning quietly, I shake my head at the overexaggeration.

I need this session. I know I do.

Stupid Joey. Stupid me for wasting two years with him. The worst part? I'm obsessing over what *I* did wrong.

What did you do wrong, Jett?

Nothing. Not a damn thing.

I have yet to give my best friend any details about what happened the day my ex left. I understand my brain well enough to know that I should talk to someone sooner rather than later, but I'm just not ready to share any of this with someone I know.

At least not with McKenna.

Definitely not with my brother, the only other constant in my chaotic life. Those are the only two people I could talk to. How sad is that? My dad doesn't need the stress of his grown daughter's breakup when he is two states away. My mom would just try to force me into more therapy if I mentioned my state of mind.

As the doors of the elevator close behind me, I lean my head back against the metal wall, taking long, slow breaths. The quiet instrumental music sounds like something from my teenage years, and I can't help but nod along to the beat, letting some of the tension slip from my shoulders. No one was paying the weird, wet girl any attention in the lobby, but my brain is convinced that everyone was judging me.

Like anyone would want to look at this hot mess.

I tap my foot to the beat of the music pouring out of the speakers, relaxing more with each passing floor until the song cuts off mid-note. The elevator shutters a few seconds later and comes to a sudden halt, jarring me into the control panel. At first, I assume someone is about to get on with me. I close my eyes and lean against the back wall, willing myself to breathe through the anxiety of sharing a small space with random strangers. Except, why would the music have stopped?

My heart races against my chest at the realization that the elevator is no longer functional. I'm trapped in this metal death can. I slam the call button with my palm, but nothing happens. I press it again. And again.

My fingers tangle into my hair, pulling on the loose strands.

"No, no, no, no, no. This is not happening right now."

Slipping my phone out of my back pocket, I'm torn between calling McKenna to panic or contacting the office a few floors above. It's pointless, though, as there is zero cell service in here. Zilch. Nada.

Desperate, I hit the alarm button. A shrill chime fills the metal contraption and the surrounding elevator shaft. I pace in the small space, counting my steps while trying to keep my breathing even. Three steps across, pivot, three steps back. I hate that it's an odd number, but changing the rhythm of my footfalls to adjust the number of steps feels too unnatural.

"Well, Jett. If you'd stuck with your plans out of high school to move to Kentucky and open a bookstore, you wouldn't be in this mess," I mumble to myself. "You could be living a quiet life in racehorse country instead of dealing with heartbreak."

One hundred seventeen steps around the elevator later, a literal voice from above nearly scares the shit out of me.

"Anyone in there?" the deep, gruff voice asks.

"Yep," I squeak, a hand clinging to my chest in an attempt to keep my pounding heart from taking a leap.

"Anyone injured or need medical assistance?"

I blink a few times, still trying to fight off the uneasy feeling of being trapped in this tube of death. "Um, no. I'm the only one in here. Scared shitless and could use a shot of whiskey, but I'm not injured."

It sounds like the guy chokes back a laugh. I'm glad someone finds me funny, because I sure as hell don't.

"Lucky for you, I was a few floors above you working on a different issue. Same elevator bank, so I heard the chime as soon as you triggered the alarm."

"Lucky isn't the word I'd use," I say breathlessly as the singular thought of being trapped continues swirling around my brain. Trapped. In a metal box. Hundreds of feet up. "If you were close, why'd it take you so long to get over here?"

A solid thunk above me triggers the most undignified squeal—I don't have anyone or anything to blame it on except that my nerves are shot.

"No reason for panic, ma'am. Storm just knocked out the power, and the generator didn't transfer. Besides, ten minutes is better than the two hours it'd take the fire department, yeah? I'm going to drop onto the roof of the cab so that I can open the doors and help you step out, okay? The elevator may shake some, but you're safe."

I hum a response but still jump a little when I hear and feel him land on the roof above me.

"Still with me, ma'am?"

"Mmm, yep."

"Want me to walk you through what I'm doing?"

"Sure. Why not?" Mumbling more to myself than to him, I add, "Nothing else to do."

He chuckles, his voice trickling down to me. "Are you always this spicy? Or just today? You're stuck between floors, so I'm going to disable the door restrictor and then manually roll open the car doors. You're only a few inches above a floor, so you'll be able to just step out."

Moments later, the doors to this stupid contraption open to the most ruggedly handsome man I have ever seen.

"Holy fireballs."

The words slip out before I can stop them. He looks at me somewhat perplexed, like there's no way he heard me correctly. But hot damn, this guy is worth looking at. If he were a book boyfriend, his defined, scruff-covered jaw and dark, chocolate eyes would melt the panties right off the female lead in any less-freakishly terrifying moment. Even covered in what looks like soot, this guy is love-interest quality. Dark-brown hair peeks out from the ball cap he's sporting, and his cotton uniform shirt clings to mile-wide shoulders. I wonder what they'd be like between—

No, Jett. Do not go there.

He's not insanely tall—maybe five-foot-ten—but the space he consumes makes me feel tiny in comparison. I swear I am trying to keep my eyes on his face, but they apparently have a mind of their own as they roam my rescuer's fine form. When I finally force them up north, I nearly choke on an embarrassed laugh as I realize he is staring at me with a mix of what I think is amusement and bewilderment.

Damn it, Jett. Quit staring.

I clear my throat before finding my voice. "Thanks for, you know"—I motion behind me at the still-open elevator—"that, and all. Though I guess it's probably part of your job. Otherwise, how would you know that stuff, right?" I groan, darting my eyes all around us, terrified of landing them on the scrumptious man who just saved me. "Sorry, I ramble when I'm nervous. Or stressed. Or really any time."

Shut. Up. Jett.

"Noah." The tin can hero holds out his hand as he introduces himself. "And it is in my job description, but you are very welcome."

I slip my hand into his much larger, much rougher hand for only a moment before I pull back and begin fidgeting with the hem of my shirt.

So late. So, so late.

Shit. McKenna is going to kill me. Not really—she loves me too much—but we made a deal last night that I would make it to this appointment today and she would ask the single dad of one of her preschoolers out for coffee. I want my best friend to find her person even if I can't find mine.

I need to get upstairs. And far away from this hunk of a man before my brain turns to mush and I make a fool of myself by drooling.

"I need to get up to the twenty-seventh floor. Where is the staircase?" I rush, looking around.

He points to the door at the end of the elevator bay. "Through that door. Each flight is numbered, so you shouldn't have any issue finding twenty-seven."

I thank him and practically race to it. As the door to the staircase closes behind me, I can't help but think that I wouldn't mind running into Noah again.

***

"I am sorry, Miss Taylor. You missed your session by over half an hour, and our next opening isn't until tomorrow."

Of course, the power was restored while I was racing up the stairwell, so the computers were up and running in my therapist's office by the time I made it to their floor.

"I've been here, though," I plead, my hands clenching and unclenching as I try, and fail, to keep it all together. "I was stuck in the elevator and had to wait for help."

"I understand that, ma'am. However, we only had a thirty-minute appointment set for you today, and the patient following you was on time for hers."

My eyes close in defeat, the weight of all the recent drama in my life once again crushing me. My voice is nearly a whine as I ask, "Is anyone else available to meet with me today? I'll wait all day if I have to."

The receptionist looks at me with a mix of pity and annoyance but sighs before scrolling through the appointment app on her computer. The second sigh that leaves her lips tells me everything I need to know. "I am sorry, but it looks like everyone is booked up."

My shoulders slump as my chin trembles, this morning's insanity finally clashing with my own chaotic thoughts.

I'm making my way toward the door when the receptionist takes pity on me and says, "There is a psychiatrist who offers emergency sessions in the afternoons, if you want her contact information."

Can I set the month of January on fire, please?

Anxiety rages war on my stomach and pulse as I try to accept my reality that I am now one of those patients needing an emergency mental health session. Nibbling on my bottom lip, I nod. Pinky promises are serious business.

I can do this.

"Where is she located?"

"Havenwood."

I jolt back a little. "Havenwood?"

The receptionist nods, oblivious to my shock. "Yes, ma'am. If you make your way to I-20 and—"

"My brother lives in Havenwood. You mean to tell me that I've had a closer option within this practice for the last two years?"

"Miss Taylor, Dr. Kristen Flynn just recently transitioned to a small personal office. She is technically no longer a partner in this practice, but I can assure you she is wonderful at her job.

And she keeps afternoons open for those individuals who find themselves in unexpected situations." Her smile is reassuring, though my heart and head are anything but.

Reassured, that is.

The thought of someone new seeing inside my head is daunting. I've seen the same therapist for the last two years, having only recently admitted to some of my more intimate struggles. The ones my family doesn't know about.

What is there to see? Depression and a solid thunk when I hit rock bottom?

Eyes clenched shut, bottom lip firmly between my teeth, I nod again. "I'll take the number." No point in putting off the inevitable.

***

The trembling in my fingers almost has my phone falling to the ground as I dial Dr. Kristen Wilson-Flynn's office. I haven't made it to the stairwell yet—no way am I getting back on the elevators after the massive failure earlier. Though I wouldn't mind running into that mechanic from earlier again. I have a feeling he'll be embedded in my memories for a while.

As the phone line rings, I steel myself for someone to answer. If I wait until I am in my car, I'll chicken out. Calling strangers, scheduling appointments—I prefer to do all of that online. No need to have human interactions when it isn't necessary.

Maybe that sounds a little too hermit-y.

If the shoe fits...right?

People make me nervous. I never know how to interact with strangers, and I always zone out into a daydream when I should be following along with whatever story or tidbit is being shared.

I've never been good at friendships or relationships—not being mentally present, creating stories when I should be focusing on any given task, and not hearing what anyone says until their words process a few seconds later doesn't lead to deep connections. It wasn't until I was twenty-three and struggling with a college assignment during my final semester that I finally talked to someone about my lack of focus—or rather, hyper focus on the wrong thing—and completed an ADHD assessment. Tada. Two decades of struggles explained in an hour.

The phone in my hand quits ringing before a motherly voice travels through the speaker. "Dr. Wilson-Flynn's office. This is Willa. What can I do for you?"

Words stick in my throat for just a moment before I say, "Yes, hi. The receptionist at my regular therapist's office said you might have an appointment for me? I mean, she said you guys—er, Dr. Kristen—sometimes kept afternoons if it was important. They can't see me here today and"—I stutter over my words— "I don't know. I'm hoping you can help me out?" It ends in a question. I almost resume my rambling, but the receptionist beats me to it.

"What is your name, sweetie?"

My back presses into the wall as I try to slow my heart rate. I can do this.

"Jennette Taylor, but I go by Jett."

"Hi, Jett. Our office is right off the square in Havenwood. What time can you be here?"

"I'm about an hour away, but I can head straight there from Atlanta."

"Okay, Jett. I'm putting you down for one thirty this afternoon. Does that work for you?"

I nod, unable to believe how unfazed she is by my unscheduled, spur of the moment appointment, before remembering she can't see me. "Oh, yes ma'am. I'll be there. Thank you."

"Not a problem at all, sweetie. We look forward to meeting you."

Acknowledgements

I am beyond thrilled to get Drew and Leila's story in your hands. They've been living in my head since I was a teenager, begging to see the world. They've grown with me, evolved into the individuals you just met, battled ups and downs, and learned to truly *live*. Thank you, **READER**, for taking the time to meet them. It means the world to me.

I have the best editor in the world. Not sure how she manages to do what she does when she has clients (*cough cough* me) who shift deadlines, only send portions of the book, and ask for quick proofing.

To the babes on IG who read snippets before anyone else: You guys are ROCKSTARS!

None of this would be possible without the support of my hubby and toddlers who tolerate my random work schedule, closet office time, and Zoom co-writing sprints at all hours.

And who knows? Maybe you haven't seen the end of Drew and Leila (and Kaia) yet...

Saving Grace

Thank you for reading!

If you enjoyed Drew and Leila's story, please consider leaving a review on Amazon, Goodreads, social media, etc.

Interested in a bonus epilogue that'll be available soon? Sign up for my newsletter to know when it's available:

https://emchandlerbooks.com/landers/sign-up

Still need to read Jett and Noah's story? Get it here:

https://www.amazon.com/dp/B0D8HLH4Y3

Don't forget to follow me on social media:
https://linktr.ee/emchandler.books

Works by EM Chandler

The Havenwood Series
(Sweet, Low/No Spice Romance)
Kissing Chaos: Friends to Lovers, Elevator Meet-Cute
Saving Grace: Second Chance, Secret Baby, Cowboy
Coming December 2025
McKenna and Reese (Title TBD): A Best Friend's Brother Holiday Novella
Steele Valley Voltage Series (Winter 2026)
(Low/Mid Spice Romance)
Oakley and Silas (Title TBD): Second Chance, Single Guardian, Hockey